BETTER WITCH NEXT TIME

A WITCH IN TIME BOOK 1

STEPHANIE DAMORE

CHAPTER 1

"*Y*ou're killing me," Andrew said.

What had started as a promising relationship quickly tanked after two weeks of dating. Andrew had presented himself as a confident and smart business attorney, but he turned out to be neither. We were standing on my front porch, it was summertime, the sun was setting, and the country setting would've been completely romantic if the man before me didn't make me cringe. Andrew looked up at me with puppy dog eyes. Big, fat crocodile tears rolled down his cheeks.

I looked away. I would rather take down a murderous ghost or a rogue witch compared to having this conversation.

How in the world had it come to this? All because I hadn't returned Andrew's afternoon phone call. That was how.

"I was just worried about you. I swear, I won't call you tomorrow," he pleaded.

"That's what you said when you showed up here yesterday," I reminded him before shaking my head. It was a moot point. It wasn't just the incessant phone calls and frequent daily visits. Honestly, I should've been flattered that a guy was that smitten by me, and maybe I was the first couple of times it happened, but now I was just straight up annoyed and looking to end whatever this was between the two of us as quickly as possible. "You know what, that doesn't matter. Honestly, it's not just that. None of this is working out."

"What do you mean? I'll do better. I promise. I won't call you anymore, ever," Andrew replied, unaware of how ridiculous that sounded.

"Just trust me on this. We're too different," I said.

"I can change. Just tell me who you want me to be," Andrew offered.

There were so many things wrong with that statement that I didn't even know where to begin. So I didn't even go there. Instead I said, "No, that's not the way it works. Listen, I'm sorry, but I'm not interested in dating you anymore." It was harsh, but the guy just wasn't getting it.

Andrew tentatively reached up to brush his hand across my cheek.

I took a step back.

"Don't." I held my hands up in a stop motion, but quickly dropped them before I blasted Andrew backwards. Despite my physical restraint, my power hummed to the surface. The energy was ready to be released, charged by the emotions that hung in the air like humidity on a hot summer's night.

"But I love you," Andrew said, his bottom lip quivering.

"You love me? Oh c'mon. Two weeks, Andrew. We've been seeing each other for two weeks. That's not love. Maybe a touch of lust, but certainly not love."

"I don't need a number to quantify my feelings for you." Andrew shook his head, sending more tears falling before wiping his snotty nose on the arm of his business suit. A suit that I once thought he looked sexy in. Then I got to know him. Andrew blew his nose in the crook of his arm. I didn't think I could be any more turned off by the guy, and yet there I was.

I sighed in frustration and looked down at Agatha, my Siamese cat and familiar. I swear she was laughing. Agatha, whose heyday had been at the turn of the twentieth century, found modern dating hysterical. Especially since she didn't have to live through it. Agatha used her tan paw to stifle a laugh. I gave her my best evil eye, which only made her laugh harder. Thank goodness, Andrew was too busy having an emotional breakdown to notice.

This was hopeless. Why was I magnet for emotionally unstable men?

Then, my evening brightened as I spotted an unmarked delivery truck head down the country road and come bumping up my dirt driveway. To the average eye, the white nondescript truck looked like it could be delivering anything —flowers, food, furniture. Only I knew it was something more. Fifteen years working for the Agency of Paranormal Peculiarities and I could spot a new case coming from a mile away. A country mile, to be exact. Except when the cases just magically appeared on my dining room table. I hated when they did that.

Agatha rubbed against my leg, telling me she saw it too. Being made of magic, she could go wherever I went, including back in time (when she felt like it), which was exactly what we did for the agency. I was one of a select few witches trained to travel back in time and solve cold cases. Only they weren't cold when I arrived on the scene. Like my mother, I lived for the job, and I never turned a case down. Ever. Let's just hope I wouldn't meet the same fate she did and one day never return home.

Andrew continued to declare his love for me and beg me to reconsider dumping him while I signed for the familiar-marked package.

"You okay?" the delivery driver asked me while handing the package over. No doubt he was a supernatural of some sort. Werewolf if my nose wasn't mistaken. They always gave off a wild scent, like being in the middle of the woods after a rainstorm—earthy and animalistic. The driver eyed Andrew, who was now pacing the porch, listing his qualities out loud.

"Solid job, fast car, nice hair," Andrew rattled off.

Oh brother.

"Yeah, it's okay, I've got it," I replied, tucking the awkward-sized box under my arm. I left Andrew on the porch and went inside and put the box on the couch. Part of me thought of just locking the door, or better yet, hopping back in time to where ever this assignment took me and leaving Andrew on the porch. The only problem with that was he'd still be there when I got back.

Grudgingly, I went back out to the front porch.

I looked down at Agatha, to Andrew, and back to Agatha again. She nodded, knowing what I was about to do. I glance from side to side out of habit to make sure the coast was clear. Not that I needed to worry, living out in no-man's land here. I didn't even have any neighbors, not unless you counted the deer that nosed on through the farm fields every evening.

With the delivery driver long gone, I walked over and took Andrew by his hand. Skin to skin worked best. Andrew smiled at my contact and then his eyes rolled back, the smile momentarily replaced by a goofy grin while his mind floated off to La-la Land. I was careful to hold on for only five seconds. I didn't want to erase too much of his memory. Andrew blinked a time or two when I let go of his hand.

"I guess you should be going," I said when he looked over at me.

"What?" Andrew replied, shaking his head and trying to make sense of the situation.

BETTER WITCH NEXT TIME

"Just so you know, I completely respect that you want to date other people," I said, planting the seed in his mind where I knew it would grow.

"Date other people?" Andrew asked.

"Yes, and you're right. I think there is someone out there who is perfect for you, and I'm not her. Good luck." I took a couple of steps back.

"Er, right. Okay. Well, good night then." Andrew looked around my yard, seeming to take in the old farmhouse with its freshly-painted white clapboard siding and wide-planked front porch, for the first time. He sort of swayed a bit as he walked down the steps back to his flashy sports car.

"Do you think you might have zapped him a bit too much?" Agatha asked me.

Andrew got behind the wheel and zoned out for a second before starting the car.

"Nah, he'll be all right," I said, walking back inside the house, leaving the screen door to slap shut behind me.

"Let's see what we've got here," I said, picking up the box and carrying it with me to the kitchen table.

At about the same time, my cell phone rang. I took it out of the pocket of my jean shorts and saw that it was my best friend and fellow cold-case solving witch, Lexi Sanders.

"Was that ripple in the atmosphere you breaking up with another boyfriend?" Lexi asked when I answered the phone.

"You seriously couldn't sense it, could you?" I'd like to think my best friend was joking, but Lexi had the ability to sense things others couldn't.

"Maybe," she joked.

"Why do men have to be so...so..." I was at a loss for words.

"Clingy?" Lexi filled in.

"Yes! And just downright ridiculous. You should've seen Andrew; he was acting like a nut. I hate it. I'm just not cut out for dating." I loved men, but I hated relationships. And I didn't date warlocks. Too much of a power struggle. The fleeting image of my father, the wicked warlock, leaving my mother and running off in the wind came to mind.

"Girl, I hear you," Lexi replied.

"But things are going good with you and..." Shoot, what was Lexi's new boyfriend's name?

"Shawn."

"That's it," I said. "Sorry, my mind is so scattered. Yet another reason not to date!"

Lexi laughed. "You just haven't met the right guy yet."

"I'm pretty sure he doesn't exist. But, I'm happy things are going well with you and Shawn."

"So far. None of my scare tactics seem to be working," she replied.

"Give it time," I joked back. Agatha jumped up on the table and started rubbing against the box, reminding me to get back to it. "Hey listen, I have to run. Special delivery."

"Where you off to?" Lexi asked.

"Don't know yet. I haven't even opened the box."

"Well, take care, you. Call me when you're back," Lexi replied.

"Will do, and you know I'll fill you all in on the next debriefing." Twice a year, the agency summoned all of us time-traveling witches for a long weekend away, where we reflected on our recent cases, shared our tips and tricks of the trade, and gelled together as a team. Industry professionals had conferences; we had debriefing sessions. Personally, I liked to think of it less as a work function and more as a time to drink fruity cocktails with my girls and work on my tan.

"Where is it this time? Cabo?" Lexi asked.

"Some place like that."

"Good deal. Now go kick some butt."

I clicked off with Lexi and looked down at Agatha. "You ready to do this?" I asked her.

"Open her up. Let's see where they're sending you off to this time," my feline friend replied.

I cut the tape and dug inside. First out was a lovely kelly green dress with capped sleeves, a tight bodice and a pleated skirt. A corset, a pair of black high heels and a black leather purse completed the look. Inside the purse was a wallet with a fake ID, a handful of dollar bills and some change. Looked like this time I was jumping back with the name of Anna Yates. I know some witches, like Lexi, use her family name every time. I preferred to just let the agency assign me an identity. I pushed the clothes aside and rifled through the accompanying papers. A small gold key was tucked in a pocket envelope with an address on the outside: 505 West 85th Street, Apartment 2A, New York City. My new residence, I presumed. Then I read the file.

"A missing person's case," I told Agatha. "Irene Hendricks. It appears she walked out of her family's Upper West Side apartment and was never heard from again." I looked at the accompanying picture of a young lady with dark hair and doe eyes. *Where did you go?* I asked the photo. Of course, it didn't reply.

"And the year?" Agatha asked, jumping up on the table and nosing the box's contents.

"Nineteen fifty-eight." What did I know about New York City in nineteen fifty-eight? About the same amount that I knew about living on the Upper West Side.

Not much.

No time like the present to find out. I added the key and photo to my purse and turned to Agatha. "Ready?" I asked her.

"Pass," Agatha said, stretching out on the table, belly-side up.

"What do you mean, pass? I might need your help on this one." Everyone knew that familiars were supposed to help witches. It was part of the deal.

"You know how to find me if you need me," Agatha replied, closing her eyes and drifting off to sleep as if that settled it.

Yeah, I did know how to find her, through astral projection. But that took a heck of a lot of power and it would just be easier to have her by my side. Let's just hope I didn't need her...

I GOT my head in the game while getting ready. I had been to the Big Apple before, but I'd never worked the city as a cold case, and the fifties weren't my specialty. Most cases dropped me some place mundane, like Idaho in the seventies. But I never turned down a case. I liked to think of this assignment as a sort of promotion. The further back you had to travel, the more power it took to get there. Apparently, my supervisors thought I was ready. I wasn't going to let them down.

It took longer than I'd ever admit to put the corset on. The blasted thing had about thirty eyelets to fasten. Thank heavens I'd only be spending a week in nineteen fifty-eight. That was the maximum amount of time we were allowed to work a case, seven days. I pulled the dress over my head and smoothed the fabric out flat. It was the type of dress a girl wanted to twirl in, if I was the twirling type.

I added a couple of personal items to my issued leather purse. Things like a quartz crystal for scrying, and my tiger's eye for protection, plus the rather mundane, but necessary sleuthing items like rubber gloves. It's a sad fact, but fingerprints could track you across time.

"Guard the house," I said to Agatha. And I knew she would, seeing it was her place before mine.

Agatha opened one eye, yawned and fell back asleep. That was familiars for you.

My magic was at the ready, thanks to Andrew's recent visit. The moment I was centered, the energy flooded to the surface in a hot second. I closed my eyes and sat for a minute with the power. It snapped and crackled at my fingertips, just waiting to be instructed. I took a deep breath and, on the exhale, said the words that would take me back in time.

Crimes are unpunished
The world's not right.
Cosmos guide me into the time-travel light.
To the past I'll travel
Absent of any time ripple.
Nineteen fifty-eight is my time
to solve this heinous crime.

CHAPTER 2

*N*o matter how many times I jumped to the past, the experience always left me feeling a little queasy. Or maybe this time it was because my corset was just a bit too tight. The world spun faster than a merry-go-round, blurring the present and spinning me back to the past. It was like being on an out-of-control carnival ride. At least that's the way it worked for me. I know for some witches, like my girl and another time-traveling witch Nuala, time travel was an emotional roller coaster, resulting in tears, laughs, and anger before peacefulness washed over her and sent her back. I wasn't sure which one of our experiences was better.

I took a second to calm my stomach and take in my surroundings. Acres of trees, rolling hills, and an abnormal amount of green space came into focus with skyscrapers dominating the perimeter. I peeked out from the cluster of trees I had arrived behind. Across the great lawn, picnic baskets were sprawled out, kids were chasing one another, and mothers were pushing baby strollers. Like me, they were wearing dresses with pleats, only some topped off their look with fashionable hats and silk gloves. Beyond the lawn were lush woodlands, verdant paths, and wild fauna. The only place in New York City that housed this much nature was Central Park. But, here's the thing about Central Park—it's enormous. Well, as city parks go. You could spend a day walking around, taking in the sights, and never experience it all. Unfortunately, I didn't have a day to waste. I needed to figure out what side of the park I was on and the quickest way to get to West 85th Street.

Of course, I came out of the park at the entrance furthest away from West 85th Street. I should have focused more on traveling to the apartment building versus just thinking of New York City. I wouldn't have minded popping up right in the apartment and ready to get to work. There had to be a reason I arrived here in the park instead. One thing I've learned with this job is there's always a reason.

Back in the heart of Central Park, I could almost convince myself that I was still back in the present. Sure, the fashion was different, but nature was nature. But once I reached the street, there was no denying that this was a different time. I hailed a cab and tried not to suck in air in appreciation as the big metal automobile rolled to a stop in front of me. They just didn't make cars like this anymore. It wasn't just the size and shape of the sedan, but the colors of all the cars. Colors like Neptune Blue, Tropical Rose, Mountain Green, and Torch Red—bright blues, warm pinks, vibrant greens, and fiery reds. The shades looked nothing like the muted, masculine-painted cars that our society favored today. I eyed up the cab's canary yellow paint and the checkered-print strip that ran down the length of it, adding to the car's retro look, only of course, it wasn't retro now.

"505 West 85th Street," I told the cab driver, who was easily accessible thanks to the lack of barrier between the front and back passenger seats.

"Sure thing, ma'am." The cab slowly pulled away from the

curb and merged with traffic, which was always a nightmare in Manhattan, no matter what year you were in. "First time in New York City?" the older gentleman asked. He wore a brown cap that matched the stripes on his button-down shirt.

"What makes you say that?" I asked, curious more than anything. If something about my appearance gave me away, I wanted to know.

"Oh nothing, nothing. Just that we get a lot of visitors, that's all." The man was being polite, but I knew that wasn't it, just like I knew I wasn't going to be able to get him to spill it.

I sat back on the cab's plush bench seat and tried to get my head in the game. You had to be able to acclimate quickly when you time traveled, which is why I always had the same plan. Set up home base, check out the scene of the crime, start sleuthing. When you had only seven days, time was of the utmost value.

The cab rolled to stop in front of the address, and I rifled through my handbag, for the first time really counting how much money was given to me. Thirty bucks? Thirty bucks! That's it?! I frantically searched the rest of the wallet, coming up with maybe a couple extra dollars in change. Payroll would be hearing from me. I don't know how in the world a case manager would ever think thirty bucks would cut it for a week in New York City.

"That will be fifty cents, ma'am," the cab driver said politely.

"Excuse me? How much?"

"Fifty cents? That is, if that's all right with you."

"Yes, yes. Of course, that's all right. Here," I said, handing the man a dollar. "Thank you so much."

Okay, perhaps thirty bucks and some change would be enough. This was definitely New York City in its Golden

Age. A time where men wore hats, women wore gloves, and fifty cents got you a cab ride.

I got out of the cab and stared up at my new residence for the week. It was an impressive white brick building. The kind with a burgundy awning overhead and a matching carpet rolled out in front with a doorman waiting at the ready. On either side of the building stood potted juniper trees trimmed and tucked in ornate planters. The doorman grabbed the door's gold handle with his gloved hand and held it open for me to step inside. "Good morning, ma'am," he said with a nod.

"Why thank you," I replied. A girl could get used to this kind of living. I walked across the white marble foyer and looked for a sign for the stairs, but instead found the elevator waiting for me with another gentleman ready to greet me and take me on up.

"Good morning, ma'am," I was greeted once more. The elevator man's name was Henry, according to his name tag, and he too was wearing white gloves. I stood behind him while he closed the accordion-style gate in front of us and requested the second floor. At first, it seemed ridiculous taking an elevator one flight up, but then I remembered the role I was supposed to play. I highly doubted ladies from the Upper West Side were known for taking the stairs. Within a couple of moments, we were one floor up and I was exiting the elevator, thanking Henry for the lift.

"2 A," I said to myself, finding the door immediately to my right. I took the key out of my handbag and was preparing to open the door when I found it open for me instead.

"Oh," I said in surprise.

"And who are you?" A woman in her late fifties stood in the doorway. Her dark hair was twisted and pinned up. A pearl necklace hung from her rather elongated neck, and a matching set of earrings with an oversized cluster of pearls were clipped to her ears. She was dressed as one would expect for someone living in a luxury high-rise, with a cream-colored skirt and matching blazer. The white silk shell she wore matched the color of her porcelain skin.

"I must have the wrong apartment number. I am looking for..." My words trailed off as I attempted to think up a backstory.

"Anna Yates?" the woman asked.

"Yes, that's me," I said, remembering the name on the fake ID I was assigned.

"You're late." The woman held the door open for me to step inside.

Late for what? I thought but walked inside any way. As I did, the woman started rattling off instructions and directions, and I struggled to keep up with her.

"Here is the kitchen, of course."

I briefly glanced at the kitchen with its pink countertops, white cupboards, and mint-colored rotary phone fixed to the wall.

"And I'm told you need a room. You'll find the spare bedroom through the kitchen. Over here is the dining room, living room, my husband's office, which you don't need to worry about, and our bedrooms. Mr. Hendricks expects supper every night at seven-thirty. No later. You'll find the weekly menu in the kitchen drawer next to the phone. Stick to the menu. I believe Mary has dinner prepared for tonight, but you're going to have to confirm that. You'll find your uniform and accompanying hat..." The woman looked up disapprovingly at my rather short hair. "...laid out for you on the bed."

Suddenly I had a feeling that was the difference the cab driver had noticed. My hair. Some might call it a pixie cut or a boyish cut, and I realized how out of town I looked. Was it worth scrambling this woman's brain and working a spell to lengthen it before knocking on the door again?

Before I could act on that thought, she continued, "You'll work six days a week and you have Sunday off. Payday is on Friday."

An orange cat came out from the kitchen and meowed quizzically at us. He was fluffier than Agatha and his green eyes were majestic. "That's George. He's no bother," the woman said. George seemed to scoff at the idea of being written off as no significant importance.

The woman looked at me briefly. "Any questions?"

A million, I thought. "No, I'm good," I replied.

"Good. As a reminder, this assignment is temporary. Don't make yourself too comfortable." Again, she looked at me with disdain. I smiled cheerfully in response. It was better than blasting her backwards or jolting her neurons, both of which I was back to debating.

"Now, I'm late." The woman turned from me in the living room and called out. "Irene? Irene?" Getting no response, she huffed. "Where is that foolish girl? She knows I don't have time for this." She took a pastel pink coat from the coat closet, putting it on over her blazer and belting it at the waist even though the warm weather outside didn't call for one. "Irene?" she called out one more time before rolling her eyes. "I'll have to deal with her later. If you see my daughter, tell her I'd like to speak with her." With that, Mrs. Hendricks walked out the door and left me standing at ground zero.

CHAPTER 3

*T*he calendar in the kitchen told me that today was Monday, June 3, the day Irene Hendricks went missing. However, it appeared that her mother was just starting to wonder where her daughter was. It was just after one o'clock, which meant I should have a few solid hours to search and sleuth before the Hendrickses came home and expected dinner.

I checked in the fridge and was both relieved and disgusted to find a pre-molded mound of ground beef sitting on the shelf with plastic wrap over it. I'm not inept when it comes to cooking—far from it—but as a vegetarian, I didn't handle raw meat. If you wanted avocado toast or some sweet and spicy soba noodles or tofu prepared in any number of ways, I was your gal. Beef brisket, meatloaf, and pork chops? I didn't even know where to start. In fact, the whole concept of me being transported back in time to serve as the house-keeper, well, that was a disaster just waiting to happen. I was the most undomesticated witch in the history of time travel. I wish I could say that with one snap of my fingers, the house would start cleaning itself like the good fairies had managed in Sleeping Beauty, but domestic affairs still required manual labor such as picking up a broom or maneuvering the vacuum cleaner. Although, I was pretty sure I could make the vacuum zoom across the room haphazardly if I concentrated hard enough.

Thankfully, the meatloaf wasn't the only thing Mary had left in the fridge. The regular housekeeper had also made a plate of sandwiches, an assortment of cookies, vegetable soup, and two different salads, potato and pasta. I was eternally grateful for the woman since there was now something I could eat.

I had to put thoughts of making dinner and cleaning the house aside and take every opportunity I had to search the house before the police were called in, which I knew would be soon. Irene's file had said that it seemed Irene had simply walked out of her family's apartment one day and was never heard from again, but that didn't stop me from looking for any sort of struggle.

I went to her bedroom first to see if anything looked amiss. Not that I would know how it regularly looked, but perhaps a window would have been left open, allowing someone to enter the room, or her bedding would be thrown about, or even broken glass, say from a vanity, might litter the floor. However, when I walked into the room, it looked as ordinary as any young lady's bedroom could be. The bed was made, with a white lace shawl stylistically draped across the end. Both of her windows were locked, but they were accessible by the fire escape. And there wasn't a broken picture frame or mirror to be found.

There were plenty of pictures of Irene. Photos of her dressed in formal attire (prom perhaps?), her high school graduation portrait, and another one of her with a group of friends—two boys and a girl. I picked up the formal photo and studied Irene. The black and white photo didn't offer up many clues. Her dark hair was curled under, and her light-colored dress was strapless, with a thick sash across the bodice. Her smile was pleasant, but I couldn't say she looked happy. I put down the metal and glass frame and turned my attention to the rest of the room.

Irene's dresser and closet were both stuffed full of clothes. Seriously, I had never seen so many pastel dresses and hatboxes in my life. If she had packed a bag before high-tailing it out of town, I wouldn't have known. I then checked her bathroom. The vanity was full of facial moisturizer, false lashes, and enough lipstick to stock a department store makeup counter. Her room, like the entire apartment, looked tidy and proper, as if someone had cleaned up after the Hendrickses every single day, which is exactly why they employed a housekeeper.

I was going to have to dig deeper.

I went back to my handbag on the kitchen table and took out a pair of latex gloves. George, the cat, watched me curiously from under the kitchen table. When I looked over at him, he shut his eyes, feigning sleep. I was fine with that.

Gloves on, I headed back to Irene's bedroom.

Slower this time, I went through her dresser drawers, layer by layer, looking for any sort of clue—a key, a letter, even a ticket stub that could point me in the right direction. I went through Irene's closet in much the same fashion, hanger by hanger, hatbox by hatbox, coming up empty before looking under her bed. Finally, I hit pay dirt with the discovery of a hatbox full of just the type of clues I was looking for.

Letters.

Some were tucked in envelopes with hearts scrawled on the front, others were written hastily on scraps of paper, simple notes that read, "I miss you" or "I need to see you." I opened one of the envelopes and unfolded the note inside. It read, "To Irene, my love. I hope you don't mind that I address you this way, but that is how I feel. You are my love and I yours and I hope one day we're able to be together. Yours forever, A."

The box was full of more letters, all from A, with him professing his love and his desire that he and Irene could one day be together despite what Irene's parents may think. In one letter in particular he wrote, "I know you respect your father, and I hope one day I will be able to as well. If he would only approve of our union and allow me to be in his company, I know I could win his affections over like I have won yours."

Well then.

I put the letters back and stood, feeling as if this case wouldn't be so hard after all. The tight knot I always felt in my stomach from the moment I was assigned a case until I solved it loosened a notch. It seemed like this was only a matter of a girl who'd had enough of her family's disapproval and ran away with her boyfriend. No wonder she was never found again. She didn't want to be. And who could blame her with parents who wouldn't understand her for who she was? Or allow her to love whom she chooses? It wasn't the first time that I had tracked a missing person who had decided to up and leave their life for love. Like in those other cases, all that was left for me to do was to perform a scrying spell to track Irene down and convince her to come home. If all else failed, I could always zap her and drag her back with me, or even make her forget A. forever, but I always preferred people returning home on their own free will. More times than not, especially with first loves, the love affairs never worked out. We all know how often young love turned sour, I thought to myself, before letting it go along with the bitterness of my past.

"Now let's do some magic, shall we?"

In my experience, scrying spells always worked best when you had an object of the person you were tracking to focus on. The more important the object was to the person, the more energy they imprinted upon it, and the easier it was to find them. Bonus points if the object was made out of metal. Metal was a better conductor of energy, just like always.

I remembered seeing a jewelry box on Irene's dresser and went back to her room, opening the little wooden drawers and taking out object after object, letting them rest in my hand with my eyes closed until I found the one that felt the warmest and offered up the most energy. When I opened my eyes, I saw a heart-shaped locket with a long gold chain in my hand. I figured it was some love token from the mysterious A., but when I peeked inside the locket, I saw a black-and-white photo of a young woman. It wasn't Irene or her mother, but the family resemblance was there. I wasn't sure who she was, but she had to have been someone important to Irene. Perhaps an aunt?

I took the locket and walked across the hall to the bathroom. Like the kitchen, the bathroom was styled in mint green, baby pink, and white, though this time the cabinets were painted a milky shade of green, the bathtub and the toilet were baby pink, and the countertops were white. All of the fixtures were gold, including the palm-sized drawer pulls on the bathroom cupboards and drawers. I examined the wall-length mirror with its gold trim and little rose accented tiles and decided that yes, this mirror would do just fine for the spell I was about to perform.

Witches can scry in a couple of different ways. One required the use of a crystal, like a quartz or amethyst, along with a map. The other was to use a smooth surface, like a mirror or a body of water that you can peer into like a looking glass. That was the method I was going to try first. It required more power, but it would give me a more accurate picture of where Irene was, since I could see her in real time versus just picking up a vague location on a map. Plus, I didn't have a map of New York City on me, something I could've sent Agatha out for if she could've been bothered to join me.

I held the necklace in my hand and the chain intertwined between my fingers. Taking a couple of deep breaths, I relaxed my body and focused on the threads of energy that were bound to the necklace. In the silence I whispered:

> *Power I need, come to me.*
> *With harm to none, so make it be.*

Irene's energy glowed a soft lilac color, spinning out from the necklace in tiny wisps, thinner than a strand of hair. I followed the threads in my mind as they wove around the apartment, clustering together where she spent the most time—her bedroom, the kitchen, and one of the settees in the living room. There were two, both a golden honey color. There was a distinct absence of Irene's presence through the rest of the house, including her parent's bedroom and her father's study. In my mind, I held onto the threads as they wandered out the apartment's door and down the corridor.

I held onto that energy and pushed my mind further, urging my power to seek her out like a heat-seeking missile. The images blurred, moving rapidly, down the sidewalk, down the stairway to the subway. I couldn't tell if she was alone or afraid, just that she was on the move and quickly.

Then I opened my eyes and saw her in the bathroom mirror. I was seeing Irene as she saw herself—young and beautiful—not how she was now or where she was located.

Irene's picture came front and center in the mirror. Her skin was ivory white. Her lips were painted a rich red courtesy of one of the dozens of tubes of lipstick she had kept stocked in her bathroom drawer. And her shoulder-length brown hair was curled in the fashion of the day. I couldn't help but bring my hand up to touch the short spikiness on the back of my head and tried not to chastise myself for not thinking that part through. It would've only been a matter of a few words, a quick spell, to lengthen my hair for this assignment. Even a wig would've been smart. Although I preferred a spell. Far less itchy.

I clutched the necklace tighter in my palm and closed my eyes to strengthen my power and said:

> *Scrying secrets come to me.*
> *Show me Irene so I might see.*

I opened my eyes and watched the image swirl before me, revealing another image of Irene. Her expression was stoic, her makeup was no longer perfect, the lipstick long removed from her lips. Her hair, which had seemed so perfect a minute ago, lay flat and limp on her shoulders. I tried to expand the image to see where she was, but I couldn't. The picture remained cropped in tight, like a headshot.

And that's when the fog rolled in.

It started at the edge of the mirror, like a wisp of smoke, until it continued to build up and roll across the glass, clouding the vision.

"What in the heck is going on?" I squinted and focused my powers to no avail. Someone else was blocking my vision. Someone who was more powerful that I was.

I attempted to blow the fog back with air, and then physically, pushing against it with my hands, but there was just too much to contain. It spilled over the edges and moved around my palms, making my efforts futile. I needed another spell. Thinking fast, I called up the power of wind saying,

Wind rise up and aid me.
Clear this fog that I may see.
As I will it so make it be.

My words were useless.

The fog grew thicker and darker, swirling like an ominous storm. Irene slipped into the abyss, and that was the last I saw of her.

The front door to the apartment opened, and my heart jumped up in my throat. I thought I'd have more time before someone came home. I scrambled to open the bathroom window and fanned the fog out into the fresh summer air. A light haze still hung in the air and clouded the mirror, like smoke.

I opened the bathroom door and peered out, but I couldn't see who had come home from where I was standing. Looking down, I realized that I hadn't even changed into my uniform yet. Note to self: next time, get into character immediately. I had a feeling Mrs. Hendricks would fire me on the spot for not complying.

But she wasn't the one who was home.

Mr. Hendricks rounded the corner to the hallway. He looked to be in his fifties, like Mrs. Hendricks. He had dark, curly hair clipped short and a mustache. He wore a brown business suit, with a white shirt, and brown and mustard yellow striped tie.

I resisted the urge to duck back inside the bathroom and hide. Instead I said, "Afternoon, sir."

The man completely ignored me, his face buried in a stack of papers he held a foot from his nose, as he walked down the hall toward me and went directly to his study, unlocking the door and closing it behind him.

Nice to meet you, too.

I turned and looked at the bathroom mirror once more.

The only thing that stared back was my reflection. I thought back to what had just happened.

Who and what was I dealing with here, I wondered.

A witch? Another supernatural? Nothing in Irene's file hinted that she even rated on the magical index, but that didn't mean it wasn't possible. Magic of some sort was at play here, and I had no way of tracing it. I was going to have to track Irene down through other means and fast, because I knew for a fact her family never saw her again.

The mysterious A. from Irene's love letters was the first lead I had. But it wasn't like I could just ask the Hendrickses who he was. They didn't even realize their daughter was missing, and it would've been completely out of line for the housekeeper to pry into such private matters. Even if I had pretended to stumble across the love letters while cleaning, it wasn't my business. And I didn't want to get booted out of their apartment. As much as me being a mid-century house-keeper was a joke, it was a smart undercover gig.

Unfortunately, that undercover gig now required me to play the role that I was assigned, which meant no more sleuthing for the afternoon. For the first time, I went into the spare bedroom. It was a utilitarian space with nothing more than a twin-size bed and a dresser. I opened the dresser and found some extra clothes, most likely belonging to the regular housekeeper. However, from the sparse look of the room, it didn't look like she lived here full time like I was planning to do. The room's bedding, window sheers, and wall color were all decorated in shades of peach. The carpet was pink, like the uniform that was waiting for me to put on.

I looked at the pink dress with its white capped sleeves and matching collar and wrinkled my nose. A coordinating, lightweight white apron and small white hat—if you could even call it that, it was more tiara-like ... a princess crown of housekeeping—finished off the uniform. I quickly dressed, feeling more like I was getting ready to attend a Halloween costume party than to prepare a meatloaf. I glanced out of the singular bedroom window and saw that, like Irene's bedroom, mine also had a fire escape, which made sense since both bedrooms were on the backside of the building. I opened the window and stepped outside. The black metal fire escape was sturdy, and it would make sneaking in and out of the Hendrickses' place that much easier. Bonus points that we were only on the second floor. I felt the same way about heights as I did meatloaf—slightly nauseous.

After getting over the impressive-looking oven with its eight knobs, six burners, and two oven doors, I set about trying to figure out how to operate the intimidating appliance.

"It's not as easy as it looks," I said to George, who was staring at me from the kitchen doorway. Unlike Agatha, he didn't reply, which was slightly disappointing.

A couple of hours later when Mrs. Hendricks walked into the apartment, I was proud to say that I had managed to bake the meatloaf, peel, cut and boil the potatoes, and shuck enough peas to make a presentable side dish—and I didn't curse anyone or any appliance in the process. Mrs. Hendricks stood over my shoulder and examined dinner's progress.

"Don't forget, plated and served no later than seven-thirty," she said as she walked through the kitchen. I took that as her sign of approval, even if it was a rather rude one. Perhaps I'd get to curse someone yet.

"WHERE'S IRENE?" Mr. Hendricks asked, seeming to notice for the first time that his daughter wasn't at the dinner table.

I walked around the table, plating their mashed potatoes and spooning out peas to go with the meatloaf.

"You're just now realizing she's absent? I've been asking you if you'd seen her today," Mrs. Hendricks shot back.

Mr. Hendricks didn't reply.

"Well, have you seen her today or not?" Mrs. Hendricks asked, the annoyance heavy in her voice.

"Today? No, can't say that I have. And who are you?" Mr. Hendricks asked, really looking at me for the first time.

"Anna is filling in for Mary," Mrs. Hendricks replied for me.

Mr. Hendricks looked perplexed.

"Mary's taking care of her mother. Do you remember now?" Mrs. Hendricks asked.

Mr. Hendricks shook his head no.

"Honestly, Frank. Sometimes I wonder why I even bother."

Mr. Hendricks didn't seem to know why she did either. He returned to his dinner, forking at his meatloaf and eating in silence.

"Well, how rude of Irene not to join us for supper. She knows how much it displeases me to have her galivanting around town." Mrs. Hendricks looked to the clock on the dining room wall as if confirming Irene's tardiness. "Who's that dreadful friend of hers again? You know, the one who has a *job*." She said the word with more disdain than I'd ever thought possible.

Mr. Hendricks continued to eat.

"That makeup counter girl. You know who I'm talking about."

Clearly, Mr. Hendricks didn't know and didn't care. He leisurely ate his supper while Mrs. Hendricks' plate remained untouched.

The minutes ticked by, her food getting cold, but still she let it sit.

"The redhead. Oh, what in the devil is her name?" Mrs. Hendricks said, thinking aloud.

Again, more silence.

Finally, after Mr. Hendricks was about finished with his meal, Mrs. Hendricks said, "Penny, that's it! She's probably with that one."

Mr. Hendricks stood to leave the table, leaving his plate for me to clear.

"You're not joining me for supper?" Mrs. Hendricks asked her husband.

"You can't expect me to sit at the table all night, now can you? I have to work to do." With that, Mr. Hendricks walked out of the room and left Mrs. Hendricks to eat her peas alone.

CHAPTER 4

I woke the next morning to George pawing at my face to feed him and the Hendrickses talking somewhere in the distance. The morning had started without me, and I was going to have to hustle if I was going to pretend otherwise. I got dressed in record time, patted the back of my hair down (reminding myself why I normally loved my style), and bustled out to the kitchen to start the coffee and give George some kibble. While I checked out the contraption on the stovetop that was supposedly the coffee maker, bits of the Hendrickses' conversation floated down the hallway.

"If the Morgans find out, there's no way they're going to entertain a marriage proposal," Mrs. Hendricks said, matter-of-factly.

"What do you suggest we do, call the police?" Mr. Hendricks replied, and even I could tell by the tone of his voice that he didn't think that was a good idea.

"The police? Of course not! Don't be ridiculous. I said I didn't want the Morgans to find out. We have to be smart about this. Find her and bring her back home immediately."

"I don't disagree with you, but I don't understand how in the world you expect me to do that," Mr. Hendricks said. "I'm extremely busy at work and I don't have time to take a day off and go hunting the city for that daughter of yours."

"Don't you give me that line. She's just as much your problem as she is mine."

"This is just like her. Run off and get into trouble and expect us to bail her out," Mr. Hendricks replied.

There was a moment of silence, and I quickly went to the fridge to retrieve some eggs in case one of them unexpectedly walked into the kitchen.

"Give her time," Mr. Hendricks said after another minute.

"Time?"

"She's always come home before. This time will be no different. I'm sure of it," Mr. Hendricks said.

"If you're sure..."

"I am. Now, you go about your day. Don't let on to anyone that you're worried one bit. I'm sure Irene will be home by supper tonight," Mr. Hendricks said.

"I don't know what we're going to do with her," Mrs. Hendricks replied.

"Get her home, get her married to James, and let her be the Morgans' problem," Mr. Hendricks said flatly.

"I hope you're right."

"I am."

"Fine. I'll give her time," Mrs. Hendricks said.

"Good. Now not another word," Mr. Hendricks replied. I could tell they were walking up the hall now.

"You don't have to worry about *me* saying anything," Mrs. Hendricks said as they entered the kitchen.

AN HOUR LATER, after Mr. Hendricks had left for work

(without eating the breakfast I had prepared according to his schedule, I may add), Mrs. Hendricks followed suit without speaking a word to me. That was fine by me. I had work of my own to do. I waited in the apartment for ten minutes to make sure she wasn't returning immediately and changed out of my uniform and back into the green dress I had worn when I arrived yesterday. I plopped the bacon I had made for Mr. Hendricks' breakfast into George's bowl before leaving as well. George had meowed appreciably and rubbed himself against my leg. I swear, all that cat did was eat and sleep. I was getting slightly jealous.

Henry was working the elevator again.

"You didn't by chance see Irene leave yesterday, did you?" I asked on my quick ride down.

"Irene? No, can't say that I did, but that didn't mean she didn't," he replied.

"I'm sorry?" I asked, not following.

"Afraid the old noggin isn't what it used to be. Pushing buttons seems to be all I'm good at these days," Henry replied, tapping his head. "Sometimes I even forget what floor I'm on."

"I'm sorry to hear that. If you do see her though, and you remember, can you let me know? Her mom and dad would like to speak with her."

"Will do, ma'am."

HERE'S the thing about makeup counters in New York City—they're everywhere. Every major department store employed dozens of young women to work their cosmetic counters. Add the fact that I was looking for a girl named Penny, one of the most popular names for a young lady in nineteen fifty-eight, and you could see my struggles in finding Irene's

friend. There was a Penny at Bloomingdale's who coinciden-
tally also had a friend Irene, but not the Irene I was looking
for. Saks had three ladies by the name of Penny who worked
at the cosmetic counter, and only one of them was working.
She didn't know Irene either.

I left Saks and headed to Macy's in hopes I would get
lucky and find the right Penny. If not, I at least wasn't leaving
the store without a new pair of shoes. Note to self: Don't
walk all over Manhattan in heels. I had taken a cab to
Midtown, but after that, I had been walking from store to
store. The result? My calves would look fabulous, but my
toes were starting to cramp.

I walked into Macy's, bypassed the coat check, and
approached the first makeup counter girl who was available.

"Is Penny working today?" I asked. I was finding that it
was easier to just assume a Penny worked at the cosmetics
counter than to ask if one did.

The redhead pointed to the name tag pinned on her chest.
"I'm Penny, and that color lipstick is all wrong on you,"
she said.

"I'm not wearing any lipstick," I replied.

"I know, and what a tragedy that is. With those full lips of
yours? We could really make them shine. Here try this."
Before I could even step back, Penny was applying a warm,
rich shade of red on my lips that made my green eyes pop. I
admired the new look in the mirror and then had to remind
myself what I was supposed to be doing there.

"And I love your hair," Penny continued. "You're such a
trendsetter. Are you looking for a job?" she asked, nodding
her head encouragingly.

"Actually, I'm looking for someone. Her name is Penny
and she's a friend of Irene Hendricks?"

"Oh good gracious, what has Irene gone and done now?"

"You know her?" I asked. I looked closely at Penny and

realized that she was the same girl in one of the photos on Irene's dresser.

"Of course I know Irene. She's a hoot. That is, when she can get away from her parents, if you know what I mean." Penny then completely changed topics. "Have you tried Spring Day?" she asked, spraying a bottle of perfume in the air and eyeing a woman over my shoulder nervously.

I glanced behind me and found an older lady watching us. Her gray hair was pulled back in a tight bun. Eyes like a hawk. Her blue skirt and white blouse mirrored Penny's uniform, only hers was finished off with a suit jacket. The woman's attention darted around the floor at her employees.

I kept my voice low. "Is there somewhere we could go to speak in private?" I asked her.

"There is, but I can't leave the floor right now. That's grounds for being sent to the basement, and you don't want to go in the basement." Penny handed me the bottle of perfume to smell, a fake smile plastered to her face.

"What's in the basement?" I asked, picking the perfume up and smelling it.

"The phones, of course. Have you ever worked a switch-board at a department store?" The girl shuddered. "Besides, you'll never find a husband working in the basement." Penny was dead serious. I had a feeling that, like many girls in her day, matrimony was high on her to-do list.

"No, I suppose you wouldn't." I put the perfume down. "The thing is, she hasn't been home since yesterday morning, and nobody knows where she is. Her family has asked me to help track her down. They want to make sure she's okay."

"Irene's run off?" Penny had moved on to selecting the right shade of blush and eyeshadow to complete my look.

"Or something bad has happened to her," I said in all seriousness.

"What does Archie say?" Penny leaned in and applied a bronze shade to my eyelids.

The infamous A. "I haven't talked to him. Do you know how I can get ahold of him?" I tried not to sound too hopeful.

"I'm sure he's at work right now," Penny said.

"Which is where?"

"The newspaper stand right outside Irene's building. How do you think she met him?" Penny held up a handheld mirror for me to see my reflection. I hadn't worn this much makeup since Lexi dragged me off for makeovers on my thirtieth birthday. So yeah, it'd been a while, but I couldn't deny that Penny was gifted.

"Here, take a free sample of the lipstick with you." She put the miniature lipstick in a little paper bag complete with a piece of tissue paper. "And here's a sample of our new fragrance too." She leaned in. "I think it smells a little bit too strong for me, but everyone else is loving it, so who knows," she said, shrugging her shoulders.

"If you see Irene..." I let my words trail off.

"I'll be sure to tell her to hightail it home."

"Thanks so much, I appreciate it. All of it." I held up the bag for emphasis.

"No problem whatsoever. Thanks for stopping in."

$\mathcal{A}$s promised to myself, I did swing through the shoe department and picked up a pair of black flats, along with a pair of petal pushers and matching shirt for a whopping twelve dollars. I stepped into the ladies' fitting room before leaving the department store and traded my heels and dress for the more comfortable new outfit and shoes. Even with the new shoes, I decided to take a cab back up to the Hendrickses' apartment, knowing how reasonable the cab fare would be. I still had seventeen dollars to my name, which should be plenty for food and transportation for the next couple of days.

Once back at the apartment building, I paid the cab driver a couple of dollars and headed directly for the newspaper stand that I had previously overlooked. I stood in line behind a couple of businessmen who were completing their early afternoon purchases and took in the stand's inventory. I hadn't realized how many daily newspapers New York City had in the fifties. Not to mention the magazines and candy. The stand was a hub of information. I couldn't believe how much this would all change within a few short decades with the burst of the Internet. Kind of made me feel a bit nostalgic and wishing the Good Ole Days were still here. I was lucky in that regard. Anytime the modern world became too much, I could pop into whatever time period I wished and check out for a few days. Well, any time period up until nineteen fifty. Anything past that took some extra fire power and wasn't a trip I could manage solo. Not yet.

I checked out the stand's candy stash while thinking about how I had the best job in the world. Necco Wafers, Atomic Fire Balls, Boston Baked Beans, Super Bubble, Peanut M&Ms—plus some candy that I had never even heard of lined the front counter. Like, what was a Cup-o-Gold? For five cents, I decided I would purchase one and find out. The men in front of me paid for their purchases and stood aside, leaving me standing in front of a rather old man. His gray hair was clipped short, but his silver beard was long, as were the lines down his face. Surely this couldn't be young Irene's admirer?

"Whatcha got sweetheart?"

"Just this, and I was looking for someone named Archie? Do you by chance know who he is?"

"Of course I know Archie, but I haven't seen him. And if you do, do me a favor and tell him that he's fired," the old man grumbled.

"Fired?"

"The boy didn't show up for work again. I told him if he was a no-show one more time, he was out of a job. I'm a man of my word, unlike that young boy." The man shook his finger at me. "I need employees I can rely on. I'm an old man. I can't work seven days a week anymore."

"I guess that makes two of us looking for him," I said, handing the man my change for the purchase. "Do you happen to know where he lives?"

"If I knew that, I'd head there myself and let him have it.

Can't believe he didn't show again. Now I have to stand here all day with my gout acting up. I'm not going to be able to walk the rest of the week."

I felt bad for the man, truly I did. I wished I gifted in the healing department. My skills were more of the kicking-butt and mystery-solving type. That didn't mean I couldn't send some healing energy his way. In the meantime, I asked if he needed anything. "Do you have a stool to sit on?" I asked.

"Nah, don't mind me. I'm just a grumpy old man with a bum foot," he replied.

But I couldn't let it go. Here I was complaining about my feet hurting me, but I knew this man was truly uncomfortable. I took my candy and walked down the street to the grocery store. It was a smart pit stop, considering I should probably pick up a couple of items in case the Hendrickses returned home while I was out. I picked up a basket and walked the aisles, placing a loaf of bread inside and some cold cuts. Judging by the rate that Mary's platter of sandwiches disappeared in the fridge, it was evident that the Hendrickses were fans of sandwiches and late-night snacking. In fact, I suspected that Mr. Hendricks slept only a handful of hours a night, choosing instead to lock himself inside his study and burn the midnight oil. I had yet to find out what the man did for a living, but that was about to change. Before checking out, I grabbed a bottle of Tylenol and a cold Coke for the newspaper stand man, too. Pain relievers and caffeine were pretty much my go-to for any non-magical ailment.

The old man was chatting up another customer, still complaining about his foot, when I set the two bottles down on the wooden counter in front of him.

"Maybe this will help. Give it a try," I said with a wink. If anything, the old man would at least know that someone cared. He was speechless, but in a good way. I walked away and took the rest of my purchases with me inside the Hendrickses' building.

On the second floor, I cautiously opened the apartment door and stepped inside, thankful to be greeted by silence. It seemed that both Mr. and Mrs. Hendricks had yet to return home, and if they had stopped in while I was out and later questioned me on it, I would simply tell them that I had stepped out to run to the market, which wasn't a total lie.

I walked through the apartment just to make sure the place was empty except for George and then headed to Mr. Hendricks' study. Like always, the door was locked. Even when he was inside working, I could hear him click the lock shut behind him. I put my ear to the door, listening intently to make sure that he wasn't inside and then decided it was time for me to enter.

Thankfully, tumbling locks was Witchcraft 101. It was simply a matter of me taking a hold of the door handle, closing my eyes, and envisioning the metal pieces tumbling together, aligning to the right degree and gaining me entry. The entire process took me about three seconds. The door-knob twisted freely in my hand, and I pushed the door inward and stepped across the threshold.

What a mess, were my first thoughts. Mr. Hendricks had books everywhere—crammed onto bookcases, stacked on his desk, and even arranged in towering columns on the floor. In fact, I was convinced he had more books in his collection than even some small-town libraries. This man would love the Internet, of that I was certain. Whatever he did, he was big into research. The books were all scientific in nature, heavy into chemistry and biology, several of which were scholarly journals and hand-bound copies.

Mr. Hendricks' desk was up against the left-hand side wall. Directly across from his desk on the opposite wall was a tapestry. At first, it was hard for me to make out what it was, what with stacks of books covering two thirds of it, but I shortly realized that it was the periodic table of elements. Different colored threads were used to separate the table's categories—earth metals were embroidered in a different color than transition metals, and nonmetals such as the gases were embroidered in an entirely different color from the halogens. The result was a rich tapestry full of reds, greens, blues, and golds. While it was fascinating, the tapestry wasn't going to help me find Irene. What I needed was a clue, and my intuition was telling me that I needed to take a closer look at Mr. Hendricks' work. However, with this much paperwork and clutter, I wasn't even sure where to start. Thank goodness I'm a witch.

Once more, I closed my eyes and turned in a full circle, extending my hand out at a 45° angle as if securing the space around me a circle of light. I walked in the circle a handful of times, not enough to make me feel dizzy, but just enough to feel grounded and calm. Then I said the magic words.

Heaven and Earth I call thee,
Show me the clues that I cannot see,
to find Irene and restore her to me.

A soft, warm wind rose up around me. I opened my eyes to see the papers on Mr. Hendricks' desk rise up and swirl slowly in the air like a controlled vortex until one piece of paper left the funnel and floated to me. I looked at the paper, my fingers feeling the ridge of the official government seal, and tried to piece together what the documents meant.

It was a birth certificate, only I didn't recognize the name listed on it.

The mother's name had been blacked out. All I knew was that the baby had been born in Allegheny County on April 3, 1940. Baby Howell. Howell. I said the name out loud to myself. I knew that last name. And if I could pick up the phone and call my best friend Lexi right then and there, at that moment, I would have. Lexi was a Howell descendant. She may go by Sanders in the modern world, but she always took her family name when working cases for the agency. The Howells were powerful witches and had a long history in the craft.

I looked at the dates again. Seeing it was currently 1958, that meant the baby would be just over 18. The same age that Irene was now. Was Irene baby Howell? If that was the case, and Irene had been adopted, did she know the truth? And more than that, did that make Irene a witch? Could she be blocking her location? And if so, why?

Just another piece of the puzzle.

I walked the document back over to Mr. Hendricks' desk, where the rest of the papers had resorted themselves into their proper locations. The paper magically rose up from my hands and tucked itself back in place. That's when I found my second clue, Mr. Hendricks' checkbook. The desk drawer was pulled open, perhaps the work of my earlier spell, or maybe just Mr. Hendricks' negligence. Regardless, I pulled the binder out of the drawer and opened it up. On one side were blank checks, while on the other side were their stubs. The bills were mundane, checks for the utilities and donations to charity groups, but there was one specific paystub I was looking for, and that was for their regular housekeeper, Mary. I found several of them, and now I knew Mary's last name—Petrov. Hopefully that would be enough to find her.

Old-fashioned phone books of the 1950s were things of beauty with their thick spines that would land with a thump on people's doorsteps year after year. The Hendricks didn't disappoint; they kept a tome in their kitchen drawer next to the phone. In fact, I knew exactly where was because Mr. Hendricks' weekly menu sat on top of it.

I shut Mr. Hendricks' desk drawer and went to make my way to the kitchen when I stopped dead in my tracks in the doorway. Mr. Hendricks himself came walking into his office. We were face-to-face; in fact, we had almost collided. If there ever was a moment to freak out, this was it.

But I couldn't freak out.

I had to act fast.

I reached out and grabbed Mr. Hendricks by his wrist. The shock of finding me in his office was still plastered on his face. I felt the jolts fly from my fingertips and into his body, firing all the way up to his brain to rewire his neurons.

I held on to his wrist until his expression softened, guiding him to turn until he and I had switched spots. He now appeared to have been in his office and I had been walking in. Slowly, I let go and clasped my hands behind my back.

"You wanted to see me, sir?" I asked Mr. Hendricks innocently.

"I did?" Mr. Hendricks brain was still off in space. "I, I don't remember..." He furled his brow, and I didn't want him to struggle too hard to remember.

"You would like some lunch, a sandwich, isn't that right?" I nodded my head in encouragement.

"Yes...ah, a sandwich would be great," Mr. Hendricks said, his voice a bit shaky.

"I'll bring that in for you in just a moment." I smiled as genuinely as possible and then turned on my heel and went to do just that.

It wasn't until I had gotten a sandwich together along with some chips and an iced tea and delivered it all to Mr. Hendricks that my heart rate had finally settled back to normal. The man sure didn't keep normal business hours. I was going to have to be more careful with my snooping in the future.

CHAPTER 6

I vowed to play the perfect housekeeper for the rest of the night, not wanting to arouse any suspicion that Mr. Hendricks' subconscious might want to dredge up.

That evening, the phone rang a half a dozen times. It didn't matter who answered it, the caller always hung up. My mind raced with the possibilities—was it Irene trying to get in touch, but someone kept interfering with the call, or perhaps it was whoever had taken her, if that was the case. What was the caller's motive? Or, was it seriously just a bunch of wrong numbers?

"I'll get it," Mr. Hendricks said as the third call had come in at dinnertime. Mrs. Hendricks and I had already each taken a turn answering the phone, but once again, no one was on the other end.

"I told you to get our phone line checked," Mrs. Hendricks said. "I'm tired of this happening."

"It's not like it happens all the time," Mr. Hendricks retorted.

"Frequently enough," Mrs. Hendricks replied, leaving the conversation at that.

Tonight, there was no talk of Irene at the dinner table. In fact, outside of that one conversation about the phone line, the Hendrickses didn't speak to each other at all. I found being in their presence to be insufferable, and I had a strong feeling that Irene had felt the same way. Now that I knew Irene might be a witch, I was back to thinking that she and Archie had simply run off together to make a new life of their own. After all, he hadn't shown up for work that day either.

That still didn't fully explain the fog that had rolled in. Would Irene know how to do that? If so, she had a mentor, and I had no clue who that could be. Phone books at the time were impressive, but they weren't *that* impressive. Not only that, but Irene would have to be punching some serious power. More power than I'd ever heard a young witch possessing. The fog was a fact that I couldn't ignore, and a theory was just a theory until I had the evidence to prove it otherwise.

THAT NIGHT, I woke to the sound of the fire escape creaking outside my bedroom's open window. I had no idea what time it was since digital alarm clocks weren't a thing yet, and the room was completely dark except for the light from the almost full moon outside. I thought for a moment that it must've just been my imagination or perhaps the wind had wrestled me awake, but then I heard it again. The creaking sound of footsteps; there was no mistaking it now. I darted my head from side to side and then quietly got out of bed, backing up until I was pressed against the same wall as my window. Slowly, I moved to look outside the drapes, hoping to catch a sight of who my visitor may be. I caught a glimpse of a man just as he climbed into Irene's bedroom window.

I could've gone about this a couple of different ways; I could have rushed out of my room and thrown Irene's bedroom door open to catch the intruder in a rather dramatic fashion, or I could've even started screaming to alert the Hendrickses that someone had come into their home.

But I wasn't going to do any of those things.

No, I wanted to sneak up on this person and deal with him my way.

I opened my bedroom window up slightly further so that I could step out onto the fire escape myself. With my back against the building, I crept along until I was at Irene's window. I crouched down and peered inside, unable to see the gentleman who had entered. Had he already exited Irene's bedroom? Was he now somewhere else, roaming about the apartment? Could he be about to attack the Hendrickses in their sleep?

I ducked down into Irene's bedroom. My eyes scanned the room, looking for any sign of movement. That's when I saw him. The man was to my right and he was going through Irene's desk drawers. He was looking for something, but I wasn't going to give him the time to find it. I stalked up behind him and twisted his arm behind his back with one hand, clapping my other hand over his mouth, and whispered, "Don't make a sound. Do you hear me?"

The intruder's body jerked in surprise and then he seemed to be paralyzed in fear. He began trembling under my fingertips. I quickly realized that the man was much younger than I had initially presumed, and I had a feeling I knew who he was, but I was going to make him tell me who he was and not presume his identity.

"We're going to go back outside that window and you and I are going to have a couple of words. Do you understand?"

The young man nodded.

"Good." I dropped my hand from his mouth but still held on to his arm behind his back as I led him to the window. I had him step out first with me holding on behind him. I swore to myself that if he even attempted to make a run for it, I would blast him so fast he would think he had been struck by lightning, which would be a pretty accurate description.

Once outside, the young man immediately started apologizing. "I'm sorry. I was just trying to talk to Irene." He held his hands up in a gesture of innocence. "I swear, I just need to talk to her."

"What's your name?" I asked, even though I was almost positive that I already knew.

"Archie," the young man replied.

I was right, but I wasn't happy about it. If Archie was looking for Irene, then she hadn't run off with him. That made this case infinitely more complicated—and dangerous.

"You and I need to talk," I said. "Wait here a minute and let me change. I think you and I can help each other out."

I put on the outfit I had purchased previously that day, or make that the day before as it was now past midnight. Archie and I walked to a nearby 24-hour diner. It was the type of greasy spoon that served everyone's favorites, like pancakes the size of plates and triple-decker club sandwiches. The floor was black-and-white checkered, the vinyl booths were yellow, and by the looks of everyone's plates, the portions plenty. We sat down across from one another in one of the booths and each ordered a Coke.

"You and Irene are close, right?" I said by way of broaching the subject.

"I love her," Archie simply replied. He didn't look away or seem embarrassed, or even go in the opposite direction with the macho stance. It was just a straight-out flat *I love her*. There was such truth to his statement that it even made my cynical heart do a little pitter-patter. And that was saying something.

"Here's the thing. No one has seen her for the last two days, and her parents have no idea where she's gone off to."

"What do you mean? I don't understand," Archie replied rhetorically. It wasn't that he didn't understand, but rather that he didn't want to believe it.

"So this is where I need your help in finding out what has happened to her or where she has gone off to," I said.

"We had plans. She wouldn't have left without me," Archie said, believing every word.

Or the locket, I thought, thinking of the piece of jewelry I had used to try to scry for Irene, and now that I knew she was adopted, I think I understood why. The picture inside the locket was Irene's birth mother. I was almost positive. The young woman in the picture had certainly resembled Irene, and that explanation made sense regarding why the woman hadn't looked like Mrs. Hendricks.

As I was thinking about the locket, Archie produced one from his pocket, though this one was larger and looked more like a pocket watch. That's all I thought it was until he opened it and revealed that it was more than that—it was a watch with a lock of hair inside.

"She gave me this for my birthday so that she could always be with me," he said. "We were going to make a life for us—just us."

"That was you that called tonight," I said, thinking back to all the hang-ups.

Archie nodded. "It was our code. I'd call and hang up until she answered, but she never picked up the phone tonight. Guess now I know why."

"Archie, I'm sorry," I said.

"I knew something was wrong when she didn't meet me last night." Archie shook his head as if he couldn't believe it.

A wave of emotions poured out of him. I didn't need to be an empath to know that he was distressed.

Out of the range of emotions that played across his face, he settled on anger.

"Are you sure her father hasn't taken her off somewhere just to get her away from me? That seems like just the sort of plan her parents would orchestrate," Archie said with bitterness in his voice. That thought hadn't occurred to me, but I honestly didn't think that's what had happened. Especially seeing I knew for a fact that Irene's family never saw her again. If they had just taken her away for the summer or even a year, I wouldn't be here now. But that wasn't knowledge that I could share with Archie. He, however, was ready to take that idea and run with it. Hostility seemed to build behind every thought that he expressed as he rattled on about how much the Hendrickses didn't approve of him.

"And you!" he shot across the table to me. "Who are you anyway?"

Caught off guard by his sudden focus on me, I said simply, "I'm the housekeeper. Just temporarily, while Mary's away."

"Why do you even care then, if you're just the housekeeper? I bet the Hendrickses paid you to say this to me." Archie was practically shaking as the words tumbled out of his mouth.

I leaned across the table and softly said, "Okay ... I think we both know that I'm not really a housekeeper. And I can promise you that the Hendrickses are no friends of mine."

It was against the Agency's rules for me to say exactly who I was—a witch from the future—but that didn't mean I couldn't hint at my otherworldliness.

The levelness of my voice did more to convey my seriousness than anything else I could have done. Archie sat back, stunned with the realization that something horrible could have in fact happened to his girlfriend.

"We have to find her," he said.

"I'm trying to," I replied. "Tell me, has anything odd been going on with Irene lately?" I thought back to Irene's birth name. She was a young woman who possibly had a strong magical heritage. Surely there would be some magical sparks flying by now, if they were ever going to? Especially seeing she was in love. Emotions tended to trigger such things in young witches.

Archie exhaled, seeming to blow out all of his emotions. "I'm not even sure where to start," he said, bending forward and taking a sip of his untouched Coke. Mine was just about empty by that point, but for the advertised ten cents a glass, I could go for a refill. Archie continued, "It seems like a lot of weird stuff has happened."

"What kind of stuff are we talking about?" I asked, and I had a feeling I knew where this conversation was headed.

Archie shook his head, and I knew he was having a hard time believing everything himself. "I don't know ... she was having these experiences. Like, she could sense things before they happened. It freaked her out, and she had no idea what was going on. One time, she even said something to Mrs. Hendricks and she didn't want to hear about it at all. In fact, she completely flipped out on Irene and told her to never suggest such nonsense in front of her again. But it kept happening. She just knew things were going to happen and then they did."

"You mean she could predict the future," I said.

"Yeah, I guess, if that's even possible. Irene couldn't believe it either, which is when she started searching for answers. Her father has all those scientific books in his study, so we started going through everything we could find looking for answers, and that's when she found out she was adopted."

"She knows?" That was one thing that I didn't know for sure—if Irene knew her past.

"Oh, she knows, and her parents know that she knows too. They were furious that she was snooping and discovered her birth certificate. It didn't take much for her to put two and two together, although her parents denied it up and down. Eventually, they couldn't disprove it otherwise and were forced to confess."

"How did Irene take it?" I said, picking up my glass and signaling the waitress for a refill.

"She was relieved, I swear to you. She never fit in with her family, you know? She was happy not to be related to them. But then other stuff started happening, and neither one of us could explain it."

"Like what?" I asked.

Archie leaned across the table and licked his lips nervously. "She could make fire. Like, with her fingers." He snapped his own fingers together for emphasis.

I nodded, which wasn't the reaction Archie was expecting.

"I'm serious! I swear to you. I saw it with my own eyes." He thrust himself back in the booth and crossed his arms.

"No, I believe you," I said. "They're called Fire Starters—people who can conjure flames."

Archie's eyes went wide. "It's a real thing? Like, there's other people like Irene?"

I wasn't sure if there were other people exactly like her. Usually a witch had only one gift, like me with electricity. Sure, I could use it as a weapon to knock someone out or erase their memory, but it was essentially the same power just being used in two different ways. If Irene was a psychic and a Fire Starter, who knew what other powers she had just waiting to erupt.

We were both silent when the waitress came back to refill our glasses. I ordered a cheeseburger basket for Archie and onion rings for myself. I wasn't sure when veggie burgers had been invented, but I doubted it was here and now.

"What about Penny? She's her best friend. What does she think?" Archie asked.

"She thought Irene was with you." I thought for a minute. "Does Penny know about this?"

"Oh trust me, she knows," Archie said.

"What do you mean?"

"We were leaving here late one night," Archie said, nodding toward the diner's front door. "Penny went to walk out that door, and Irene grabbed her by the arm and threw her back. A second later, a car hopped the curb and would've plowed right into her if Irene hadn't have pushed her. Irene sort of told Penny everything after that. Turns out, it was the best thing that could happen."

"How's that?" I asked.

"Penny's a bit of a supernatural expert." Archie left it at that.

It looked like I needed to take a closer look at Irene's best friend. "She doesn't have any special talents, does she? You know, like Irene does?"

"Penny? You mean other than applying lipstick?" Archie laughed. "Not that I've ever seen."

CHAPTER 7

The next morning, I hadn't forgotten my plan from the day before to track down Mary. I also was going to stop by Macy's and catch up with Penny and see what sort of supernatural expert she was. Last night, once I was back in the apartment after leaving the diner with Archie, I retrieved the phone book from the kitchen and took it back to my room. A quick search landed me a Mary Petrov who held promise. Her home address listed her as living on the Lower East Side of Manhattan. The name and location were accurate; I just had to hope the rest lined up.

I couldn't leave yet though. First, I needed to get rid of Mrs. Hendricks. Thankfully, she had plans that included brunch with her girlfriends and an afternoon museum tour, though which museum, I wasn't sure. I hadn't cared enough to ask. I was just tap-dancing with delight that her double feature meant I could hang up this ridiculous uniform for the day. I retied the apron around my back for the tenth time that morning and tried not to count down the minutes until the misses left the building.

Finally, around nine o'clock, there was a knock at the door. I went to answer it, playing the part of the perfect housekeeper to a tee, something I knew Mrs. Hendricks would fully expect. Heck, the woman even made me put together a *refreshment tray* to offer her guest when she arrived. I had no idea what went on a refreshment tray but managed to place a couple of Mary's leftover cookies and a pitcher of iced tea on the silver tray, along with a couple of tall glasses with fancy paper straws. All that was missing was the ice. Personally, I wondered why in the world you'd need refreshments when you were headed out to brunch. It must've been a rich-person thing. Or maybe it was a Mrs. Hendricks thing. Probably both.

I opened the door and was greeted by a rather stout, older woman with thick, curly gray hair. She was dressed head to toe in dark purple and bore an uncanny resemblance to a blueberry.

"Hello, ma'am, would you please come in," I said, welcoming Mrs. Berry inside.

The woman didn't address me but instead looked beyond me to where Mrs. Hendricks was now joining us.

"Madeline, dear," she said, greeting Mrs. Hendricks with a kiss on each cheek. "It's been ages. I'm so happy you're able to go out today."

"I wouldn't miss it for the world. Here, have a seat. We have time, no?" Mrs. Hendricks replied, leading her guest to the living room.

"Well, I suppose just a minute," the woman said, handing her purple coat to me without a second glance. I accepted it, and Mrs. Hendricks eyed me as if to say, *Refreshments, now.*

"Is Irene here? James wanted me to say hello," the woman asked.

Mrs. Hendricks didn't miss a beat, even as the blush rose

to her cheeks. "Oh, I'm afraid you've missed her. She's reading in the park, but I'll pass on the hello. I'm sure Irene would love to see James soon."

I remembered the Hendricks' conversation from yesterday morning and realized this must be Mrs. Morgan, although, Mrs. Berry was a more fitting moniker. I had to hand it to her, Mrs. Hendricks could lie with the best of them. If I were Mrs. Morgan, I would never suspect a thing. Of course, that only made me more suspicious of the woman. What else was she capable of lying about?

"Is that my Georgie-worgie? Come here, sweetheart," Mrs. Morgan said to George. The cat was sprawled out on the carpet, lying in a sun patch radiating in through the living room window. At Mrs. Morgan's request, he closed his eyes. "Oh, now isn't he just precious! I love cats, as you know. So does James. I told him he must meet George. He's a handsome fellow!" Mrs. Morgan continued with her sweet accolades while George pretended to ignore her. But if he was like every other cat I knew (familiar or not), he was listening and loving every minute of it. Mrs. Hendricks' lips were pulled taut in a strained smile. She obviously didn't share her friend's sentiments.

The women chatted for thirty minutes over their cookies and tea before finally heading out. Of course, not before requesting that I fetched and assisted them with putting on their coats. I barely waited for the front door to click shut before racing off to my room and changing.

Macy's was on the way to the Lower East Side, seeing it was more in Midtown and the prospective Mary's apartment was further south. I opted to take the subway this time after discovering fares were only fifteen cents each way and I preferred to save my cash for emergencies—like needing another new pair of pants. I had a feeling this case was going to cut it down to the wire. I couldn't keep wearing the same two outfits, and the extra clothes in the dresser left something to be desired.

I rode the rails to Herald Square, where I exited and headed up to Macy's. Unfortunately, when I entered and walked into the cosmetic section, Penny wasn't in sight (but her uptight manager was). I played the role of the customer, walking up to another makeup girl and asking if Penny was working.

"Which Penny?" she asked with a genuine smile.

"Oh, I don't know her last name. Red hair. Does a heck of a job with the makeovers. Can pick out the perfect shade of lipstick in two seconds flat," I replied with a smile.

"Oh, that's Penny Adams." The girl leaned across the counter. "She doesn't work here anymore."

"What? I just saw her here yesterday."

"I know. Shocked us all when Ms. Finley said she wouldn't be on the floor anymore. Penny loved working here."

"Any idea what happened?" I asked.

"No clue. I worked with her last night and she said she'd see me tomorrow. It's not like Penny to just not show. I hope she's okay."

"Me too," I said, an uneasiness settling in my veins. This case was one dead end after another. I just hoped it wasn't one dead girl after the other.

I RODE the subway further south, having looked at the station map ahead of time and knowing to get off at Grand Street, and planned on walking the rest of the way.

The Lower East Side was a far cry from the glitz and glam

of the New York City I had just left. Lower Manhattan was Old New York. I had thoughts of stopping by to see the iconic World Trade Center Twin Towers, but it was quickly evident that they hadn't been constructed yet (even if some of the other iconic landmarks were—I'm looking at you, Wall Street). It was hard to believe the transformation that took over the tip of Manhattan decade after decade. About the only thing that seemed to stay the same were the street names. The grid-like pattern that ran throughout Manhattan made it easy for me to keep track of where I was at and which way I needed to go. I walked the streets awestruck by the charm of Old New York. Street vendors sold things like shaved ice and pretzels, some stores—like Greiff Wines—had Hebrew writing on the windows, and what in the world was a haberdashery? Most of the buildings appeared to be five or six stories tall. Clotheslines zigzagged between buildings, with the morning's wash hung out to dry. Some buildings had first floor businesses, other were completely residential, like the prospective Mary's place.

I walked inside the flat-faced, red-bricked building and took the stairs to the third floor. No doorman or elevator here.

A middle-aged woman opened the door after one knock. Her ash blonde hair was twisted up in a bun. Cornflower blue eyes looked up at me expectantly.

"Hi, I'm looking for Mary Petrov?" I asked.

The woman looked concerned. "I'm Mary. Is something the matter?"

"The same Mary that works as the housekeeper for the Hendrickses?" I asked.

"Yes, that's me."

"Really? That's great. Okay." I took a second to compose my thoughts. For some reason, I was expecting Mary to be younger than me, perhaps a woman in her twenties, but this lady was probably ten years older than me, putting her in solidly in her forties. "Sorry, no, nothing's the matter. Well, something *is* the matter, but I'm hoping you can help me. My name is Anna Yates. I'm covering for you as the housekeeper at the apartment. Can I come in?"

Mary looked hesitantly over her shoulder and then back to me. "Sure, just give me a minute. My mother's not well, and I'd like to let her know we have company before having you walk in."

"Oh sure, no problem." I stayed on my side of the door while Mary talked to her mother. She was back in a moment.

"Come on in. Why don't you join me in the kitchen?" The apartment opened to the living room, which you had to walk through to reach the kitchen in the back. A bedroom and bathroom were to the left.

Inside the apartment, the lighting was dim. Mary's mother was resting on the couch, a quilted blanket tucked to her chin, a cup of tea on the coffee table in front of her. The black-and-white television, which looked more like a wooden box with two knobs and four legs, was on for her to watch, the volume set low. The old woman offered up a weak smile as we walked past, which I returned as I followed Mary on through to the kitchen.

The kitchen was something else entirely. Sure, it was small, with little counter space, but it was full of light and life. Miniature clay pots dotted the windowsill, herbs and flowers overflowing the containers. More flowers—daisies— sat in a vase on the kitchen table. On the stove, a stockpot of soup simmered, chicken noodle by the smell of it. I smiled despite my best effort not to. Mary was a kitchen witch, whether she knew it or not.

What's a kitchen witch? Basically, the Betty Crockers of

the witchcraft world. Some people think they're just talented in the kitchen and know how to work the rolling pin, but usually it's more than that. Their homemade soups really do cure colds, their teas are as good as any medicinal tonic, and their desserts really are sweeter. A kitchen witch can instantly turn a house into a home.

"What's the trouble with the Hendrickses?" Mary asked, setting a special blend of her tea before me. I had never been much of a tea drinker, but the floral aroma drew me in and compelled me to take a sip. It was sweet and light and unlike any other tea I had previously tried. If all tea tasted this wonderful, I would hang up my coffee cup for good, or at least every now and then.

"It's Irene," I said.

"Oh no, what now?" Mary took a seat across from me at the little table.

"The thing is, she hasn't been home. In fact, no one's seen her since Monday. I was hoping she might have said something to you, or that you might have an idea where she may have run off to?" I asked, taking another sip of my tea.

"Run off to is most likely what she's done. She didn't necessarily get along with her parents and it's only gotten worse as she's gotten older and turned into a young woman." Mary's comment compelled me to ask just how long she had been the Hendrickses' housekeeper.

"Twenty years this past spring," she replied with pride in her voice. I would be mighty proud of myself too if I had served the Hendrickses for twenty years and hadn't throttled either of them or turned one of them into a toad. Mary's service was commendable, and I told her as much.

"So you've known Irene her entire life then," I said.

"Since the day the Hendrickses picked her up," Mary replied.

"You knew she was adopted?"

"Of course I knew, but that's not a housekeeper's secret to tell. Words to live by, if you hope to be in the trade for long." Mary raised her eyebrows.

I didn't respond to that. Instead, I asked, "You really think she might have just run away?"

"If I was a betting person, that's where I'd place my money," Mary replied.

"But her boyfriend ... he claims she wouldn't have left without him."

"Are you talking about Archie? Or was it Isaac or Jeremy?" It was my turn to raise my eyebrows. "Irene wasn't exclusive with any one boy. They all knew how to climb up her fire escape."

Oh my.

"Mary dear, may I have some more tea?" Mary's mother's wobbly voice asked from the living room. Mary didn't respond verbally, but instead went to retrieve her mother's cup, returning and pouring out the same tea that she had just served us, but then reaching up in her cupboard to retrieve a couple of dark brown glass bottles. "My advice to you," she said while putting a couple of drops of one medicine and a drop of the other into her mother's tea, "is don't get involved. It's the housekeeper's code of ethics to keep her family's secrets. It's not her place to solve them." Mary had no idea that it was in fact my job to solve this secret, but I wasn't about to tell her that. Instead, I thanked her for her time and her tea and prepared to leave.

"Oh, and thank you so much for stocking the fridge. It's been a huge help as I learn my way around the place," I said.

"I'd offer you some soup, but it's Wednesday." Wednesday was breaded pork chops for dinner. "But, I do have a pie you can take. Mr. Hendricks loves strawberry pie."

"You're gifted in the kitchen, you know that?" I said,

taking the pie that would rival that of any New York patisserie.

Mary blushed. "It's a gift, I guess. Besides, mother will never eat all of this and heaven knows I shouldn't."

Then I thought of one other thing. "Hey, what do you know about treating gout?"

CHAPTER 8

*A*s I rode the subway back to the Upper West Side, I sat and analyzed what I knew to be true. One, Irene was missing, that was a fact, but whether it was on her own accord or she was taken by someone was still yet to be determined. Mary thought Irene was a runaway, which was very plausible given her relationship with her parents. Of course, Archie believed with his whole heart that Irene wouldn't have left him. I had believed him too, but after talking to Mary and her comment about the other men in Irene's life—well, I wasn't so sure.

Next, was Penny. Where had she run off to? She was one heck of a makeup girl, and I couldn't see her just dropping a job like that. Then there was Archie's supernatural comment. How did Penny come by her knowledge? Personal experience, perhaps?

Then you had Irene's parents, whose concerns were purely selfish. That is, they didn't care what had happened to Irene; they only cared who found out about it. That was just cold in their own right. They raised Irene as their daughter, adopted or not, and one would think that they would care about her safety. Could someone really be that self-centered?

Lastly, there was the witch connection. How much had Irene discovered? Did she know her biological family's heritage? Maybe she left home to figure out the truth and something bad happened to her along the way.

I stopped by the newspaper stand in front of the Hendrickses' building to grab a map and drop off the tonic Mary had whipped up for me. The same old man was working the stand, but at least he wasn't grumpy anymore.

"Thank you, young lady. That was mighty nice of you yesterday," he said.

"Feel any better?" I asked.

"Not really," he replied with a laugh.

"Well, here, hopefully this will help." I handed him the dark brown bottle with a rubber stopper. He took it and held the bottle up to the light. "A friend of mine is a gifted healer and said this would help." I almost said a gifted witch, which wouldn't have been good.

"What's in it?"

Good question. "I think she said apple cider vinegar, lemon juice and turmeric? She said to drink one teaspoon three times a day."

"Huh, haven't tried that before. Guess we'll see how it works," he replied. "Did you ever find Archie?"

"I did. I didn't tell him he was fired though, sorry."

"That's okay. He still hasn't showed."

"Well, I hope you find someone to help you out soon and that you feel better," I said, before heading inside to the Hendrickses' apartment. I was tempted to pick up another Cup-o-Gold, which had turned out to be a chocolate cup filled with marshmallow, almonds, and coconut, but decided it wouldn't be good for my waistline to snack on that and Mary's strawberry pie.

BACK AT THE APARTMENT, I put the pie on the counter and figured I'd had at least another hour before Mr. or Mrs. Hendricks came home. Of course, with Mr. Hendricks' schedule, there was no guarantee what time he would walk through the door. I was going to be more careful this time. George came out of the bedroom, meowed pathetically, and started pacing in front of his bowl, which was empty.

"It's not dinnertime yet, buddy," I said, bending down and scratching the cat's ears.

George bumped my hand in response.

"You have to wait a little bit longer to eat," I said as if I was talking to a little kid.

George turned and nipped my hand in response before running off. Apparently, he hadn't liked that answer.

Not wanting the cat to retaliate by peeing in my shoes, I took a piece of deli ham from the fridge and added it to his bowl. George quickly came scampering back and dug right in.

Now it was time to get to work. I made sure the map I bought showed all five of New York City's boroughs. I was going to try to scry for Irene once more, but this time using my quartz crystal and the map to guide me. I tucked myself away in my bedroom. The door didn't have a lock, but I performed a quick spell so that no one could enter the room until I released the bond. Like before in Mr. Hendricks' office, I took a moment to ground myself and to let my powers awaken. The map was laid out on the bedroom dresser, and I stood before it, my quartz crystal dangling above it, tied to a black ribbon.

Powers I need, come to me.
Show me Irene so that I may see.

The crystal swayed in a gentle gliding motion, like the pendulum on a grandfather clock, slow and rhythmic until an unseen force took over and snatched the ribbon from my hand. The crystal ricocheted across the room and smacked into the window.

"Holy cats!" I ran over to examine the window and sure enough, there was a chip in it. Thank heavens it left it at that and hadn't spider cracked rest of the window. Right now the window just looked like it had been hit by a rock, which of course, it had, except this one came from the inside area. I retrieved my crystal and examined it, noticing that it had been fractured as well.

It was official. Irene had either fully come into her magic or someone magical was hiding her.

Was that other someone magical Penny? And was she friend or foe? I no longer knew what to think. Hopefully, if Penny was with her now, she wasn't being cloaked as well.

I took a few calming breaths and opened the bedroom window to let in some fresh air and energy with it. I needed to get my mind back in the game and ready to try scrying again, this time for Penny. A few minutes later, when I finally felt at peace and ready to try again, I repeated the spell, replacing Irene's name with Penny's. Like before, the crystal began to swing like a pendulum between my fingers until it swung in an arching motion, the circle becoming tighter and tighter, zeroing in on a neighborhood. The crystal dropped, and I looked to see where it had fallen. Even damaged, the crystal pinged Penny's location within a couple of seconds.

"Harlem," I said aloud.

What was Harlem like in the 1950s? Specifically 125th Street in East Harlem? This was one time that I wished I could pick up my phone and Google something. Sure would've made life a heck of a lot easier. Regardless, it looked like I'd be paying the boroughs a visit tonight. That is, after I baked some breaded pork chops. That thought made my stomach turn. At least Mary had provided dessert.

~

LATER THAT EVENING, after all of my housekeeper duties were done for the day, I checked in with the Hendrickses to make sure that they didn't need anything else before telling them that I was retiring to my bedroom for the evening. I knew for a fact that Mrs. Hendricks wouldn't come out of her room after her hair rollers were set. Just like I knew that Mr. Hendricks would be tucked away in his study for the next several hours.

I waited until they were settled for the evening before bringing my map out once more. Again, my crystal picked up Penny at the same location. It was time I headed there myself.

I changed out of my housekeeper uniform and into a pair of black petal pushers and a cranberry-colored shirt with black ballet flats on my feet before climbing out my bedroom window and down the fire escape. I was hoping that at this time of night, the map had pinpointed Penny's apartment, or another place where she and Irene could be staying in together. Perhaps a hotel?

The subway was now my friend, so I rode it north to East Harlem, making sure to keep track of the stations and watch for my exit.

The graffiti on the subway station stairwell should've been my first clue that this wasn't necessarily the best neighborhood in town. I didn't even reach the top step before my powers were crackling and popping at the ready. I was going to take calming breaths to tuck them back in until I thought that maybe I should trust my intuition and keep them at the ready.

When the street-level air hit me, I knew exactly the cause of my uneasiness. Shifters. Their scent was heavy in the air, and I had a feeling I knew where it was coming from.

Across the street, diagonal from the subway station, was a billiard hall. Outside, a group of men stood, smoking ciga-rettes and taking drags off their bottles of beer. The air seemed to vibrate in front of them as if they could transform at any moment, when in reality they could. Tomorrow was the full moon. The true shifter could shift anytime of the month, but they had to on the full moon. Which meant, in twenty-four hours, I wouldn't want to be walking these streets alone. Well, I could hold my own, but you know what I meant. Unfortunately, the billiard hall was exactly where my crystal had pinged Penny. Shifters were physically strong, and even though magic ran through their veins, they weren't witches. I had to be smart and use the powers given to me to search the building.

Time to get my game face on.

I walked past the group of guys with my shoulders set and my eyes straight ahead. The billiard hall door was solid metal except for a little square hole cut out on the front of it where someone could look out. More shifters were inside, mixed in with a few regular humans.

The floors were charred black and the air filled with thick smoke. Balls cracked as they were hit with cues, spinning across the green felt, ricocheting off one another, and careening into the pockets. There weren't any booths, only a few scattered high-top tables filled with beer bottles and dirty ashtrays. People seemed to prefer to stand or mingle around the billiard tables. To my right, across from the bar toward the back of the room, was a set of stairs. They weren't hidden; anyone could go down them it seemed, that is, once you got past the guard. With his shaved head and strong, broad shoulders ripped with more muscles than one man should possibly have, the man was a werewolf for sure. They made the best guards. If Irene and Penny were being held here, you could bet he was the gatekeeper.

I went up to the bar and ordered a beer, trying to blend in against the wall while I watched the scene. Every few minutes or so, a man, sometimes accompanied by his date, would go down into the basement. Waitresses seemed to float up and down the stairs, delivering drinks nonstop. More people went down the stairs than came back up, that was for sure. I didn't know what exactly was going on down there, but I needed to find out. I looked for someone who I could pump for information, knowing I could erase their memory if need be. I doubted Mr. Werewolf was going to tell me what I needed to know. Just because he was bulky didn't mean he was brainless.

It took about twenty minutes, but I finally found my target. A woman came up from the basement with her date. Her floor-length brown fur coat looked way too classy for a billiard hall in Harlem. Not to mention that it was summer, and the temperatures were still sitting in the seventies. It looked like they were ready to walk out the door until the man excused himself to use the restroom. The woman took a pack of cigarettes out of her purse and I made my move.

She had the cigarette to her lips and went to light it when I said, "Mind if I bum one?"

"Mind if you don't? Johnny lost his shirt down there. He's gonna be smoking all my cigarettes until payday. Actually, you know what? Scratch that. You can have two." She gave a throaty laugh and shook the pack until two cigarettes rose up. She turned them toward me to grab. I tucked one behind my ear and put the other one between my lips. The woman flipped her lighter and held it up for me. I lit the cigarette and tried not to cough on the inhale. That wouldn't have been cool at all.

"You play?" she asked, nodding over to the stairwell.

"Not usually, but I might tonight," I said bluffing.

"Well, I hope you do better than Johnny. He got screwed, even with the flush. Word to the wise, the cards are favoring the house tonight."

"Good advice, I'll keep that in mind." The woman's date walked our way, and she went over to meet him without saying another word. I watched them leave and then walked up to the bar and put the cigarette down in the arch of the ashtray, leaving it to burn itself out. And then I thought to myself—money, cards, flush—poker.

The bartender started filling a drink order, popping off bottle caps and putting the beers along with a couple of high balls and short tumblers on a serving tray. The moment the bartender turned around, I put my own beer bottle down on the bar and picked up the tray, heading directly for the stairs. The werewolf didn't even look at me as I approached. He absently moved to the side, so I could make my way past him.

The upstairs wasn't nearly as crowded or as smoky compared to the scene in the basement. I'd guess that there were easily a hundred people hanging out in the lower level, tucked in around card tables and standing around taking in the action. Nickels, dimes, and dollar bills were at the center of each table as the card players placed their bets and the hands were dealt. I had been right; they were playing poker. I didn't know New York City's gambling laws, but I got the distinct impression that this sort of activity was illegal.

A picture had started to form in my mind, and it wasn't very pretty. If Irene really could predict the future, then she would be a huge asset to the shifters' undercover poker operation here. It made their motive for kidnapping her jump up right to the top.

Across the floor, a man signaled to me, and I assumed that he wanted one of these drinks. He was older, I'd say in his sixties. His salt-and-pepper hair was combed over and gelled in place. He had unbuttoned and rolled up his dress shirt sleeves, revealing impressive-looking tattoos on his forearms. The alpha vibe rolled off of him in waves.

"Where's Ronnie?" the man asked me when I reached him.

"She should be down in just a second," I replied, even though I had no idea who Ronnie was. "These your drinks?" I asked. I guessed and placed the short tumbler of whisky down in front of him, taking the empty one in the process.

The man latched onto my wrist. "And who are you?" he practically growled. He looked over his shoulder and I knew he was looking to signal one of his goonies to come and snatch me up. All he needed to do is make eye contact with one of his men, and I would be in trouble. This man was the boss, of that I was certain, and he knew that I didn't work for him.

With one hand holding a tray full of drinks and the other hand caught in his grasp, I used my magic to send a jolt of electricity through our connection and rewire his memory. Unfortunately, the man held on a few moments too long. I swore smoke was about to start curling out of his ears. I yanked my hand back before he could start drooling and used both my hands to steady the tray. The man stared up at me completely dumbfounded.

"Thanks for hiring me tonight. I really appreciate it," I said, and then passed out the rest of the drinks and hightailed it away from the table before anyone else got suspicious of me.

"You okay, Jim?" one of the other card players asked the Boss Man.

I exhaled and looked around the room.

I was going to have to cut this waitressing shift short. I didn't have time to mess around, I needed to find Penny and Irene and get the heck out of there before anyone else got suspicious. For all I knew, Mr. Boss Man didn't even know he was a shifter anymore. That would be one heck of a surprise come tomorrow night.

Speaking of surprises, in that moment, I spotted Penny.

She wasn't with Irene, that was for sure. In fact, at that moment, I doubted she cared much about her missing friend at all. She appeared to be on a date by the way she was flirting with the guy sitting next to her. Her date was about her age, in his early twenties. She was playing poker, or throwing out the guy's cards for him anyway, laughing, tossing her hair over her shoulder, not having a care in the world.

This opened up another slew of questions in Penny's involvement.

Did Penny know she was in a shifter bar?

Back up ... did she even know that shifters existed? If Archie was right, and Penny was a supernatural expert, then yes, she knew all about shifters.

Did that mean she could be in on Irene's disappearance?

Once again, I needed to talk to Penny one on one.

But not in here.

I took my empty tray and walked back upstairs, past the werewolf gatekeeper, and dropped the empty tray on the bar before making a beeline for the door. I had decided that I was going to stake out the billiard hall and wait for Penny to emerge. As soon as she did, I was going to follow her and make her talk to me.

Now, I waited.

CHAPTER 9

*I*f a neighborhood could be described as seedy, this one was it. Cars were scarce and rusty. Feral cats were plenty. Street lights were optional. Large tuffs of grass sprouted up in the cracks on the sidewalk. Trash littered the streets and blew against the buildings, getting caught in darkened corners.

It's a heck of a lot harder to do a stakeout when you don't have a place of residence to spy from or car to seek shelter in. There were only so many doorways I could stand in and for so long without drawing attention to myself, especially in this part of town, where shifters seemed to be congregating everywhere and more than one homeless person was looking for a place to rest. It had been close to two hours, and there still wasn't any sign of Penny or her date.

I was getting restless. I scanned the neighborhood once more. The only other business besides the billiard hall was a convenience store at the end of the block. It had been hours since I'd last eaten and I was thinking a snack was in order; after all, snacks were mandatory when you were on a stakeout.

If this had been modern day, the convenience store would have bars on its windows and make most of its money from selling beer and scratch-off lottery tickets. But, seeing this was the fifties, the store was stocked with more soda than alcohol and the only thing the windows bore was my reflection. A nice, older man, I'd put him somewhere in his mid-seventies, was working behind the counter. His hair was white, his skin dark, and his glasses were wire framed. He had on brown dress pants and a short-sleeved dress shirt with little brown diamonds on it that matched his pants. The man's clothes were neat and clean, and he looked far too put together to be living in this neighborhood. I suspected that he had been an area resident his entire life and decided to stay put when the neighborhood crumbled around him.

I grabbed a Coke and a candy bar and took them up to the counter.

"Any idea what time the billiard hall down there closes?" I asked the clerk.

"After I do, that's for sure. I was just getting ready to turn my sign," he replied while counting the dimes in his till.

"Well, I guess it's a good thing I walked down here when I did," I replied.

"That it is. I just don't stay open as late as I used to anymore. It's not worth it."

"Tough crowd?" I asked.

"That and then some. Speaking of which, you be careful out there." The man motioned out the front door. "A young lady like yourself shouldn't be walking around these types of streets alone at night. It's not safe, and tomorrow night it'll be even worse."

I took a closer look at the man, but he was as normal as a regular human being could be.

"Oh yeah?" I replied.

"I don't know what it is, but every month like clockwork,

the crazies come out on the full moon. I'm thinking about closing tomorrow night and just skipping it."

I nodded politely.

"Does make you wonder though, doesn't it?" the clerk asked, becoming philosophical.

"About what?"

"Magic, werewolves. Who knows? Maybe it's all real," he said with a chuckle.

I laughed back. "Who knows, maybe. I'll take your advice and stay away tomorrow, but since I'm here now, maybe you can help me. I'm looking for someone." I took the photo of Irene out of my purse. "Does this girl look familiar?" I slid the photo across the wooden counter. It hadn't been the initial reason for my visit, but maybe the clerk, with his keen sense, had seen something.

The man picked it up and looked at it. "No, I can't say that she does. Does she live in the area?"

"No, but I think she has friends who do," I replied, switching the photo out for a dollar bill.

"No, I don't think I've seen her, but I'll keep my eye out."

"Thanks, I appreciate it."

Another customer walked in while the clerk was making his last comment and got in line behind me. His presence put an end to our conversation. "Well, I'll let you get going now, you have a good night," the old man said.

I went to say goodbye and that was when the guy behind me pulled out a gun and put it to the side of my head.

"Give me all your money or I'll blow her head off!" he demanded. The way he delivered the line had me thinking it wasn't the first time he'd used it.

A flood of emotions ran through my veins. First was shock, quickly followed by anger, and then concern for the store clerk and the amount of distress he was exhibiting. But not fear. No, that emotion did not surface.

The clerk's hands were shaking, and he seemed unable to move. I wanted to tell the nice old man that it would be all right, but I wasn't waiting the two seconds it would take before taking this criminal down. In one swift motion, I reached up with my left arm and grabbed the wrist that held the gun to my head and twisted it, popping the gun free. It hit the floor and slid about ten feet away. Then I turned to my left so that I was facing him and with my right hand, I released an orb of electricity that shot from my fist and right into his chest. The force of it knocked him back and sent him flailing backward into a potato chip display. The man was out cold. From the store clerk's point of view, it looked like I had just punched the man and knocked him out.

I brushed my hands together and tried to shake off the extra energy like crumbs from a cookie.

"Well, I guess you can hold your own," the clerk said after a minute.

"Guess I can. Would you like me to call the police?" I offered.

IT TURNED out that wasn't necessary. A detective from the New York City Police Department walked in the door moments later. Both the clerk and I did a double-take, given that the clerk had just hung up the phone with the operator. Me, I was standing guard over the would-be robber, just daring him to flinch so I could blast him back into Never, Never Land again.

"Detective Cooper," the man said, flashing a badge at us by way of greeting.

"Vee Harper," I replied, before I thought to use my alias. I blamed my lack of thought on the adrenaline rush currently surging through my veins.

If it wasn't for the badge, I wouldn't have pegged this guy as a cop. His clothes were casual, his dark brown hair was tousled, and his face needed a good shave. Except for the eyes. No, his eyes were dark and questioning. However, that wasn't the most surprising feature of all. When I reached out and shook the man's hand, I was in for the surprise of a life- time. The detective shocked me. Literally. And not in the oh- my-goodness, love-at-first-sight type of shock. This was an honest-to-goodness electric bolt that was the equivalent of sticking a fork in a light socket. My toes tingled, and I could taste the electricity in my mouth. I was pretty sure the detec- tive's hair was standing on end. His eyes were as wide as I was sure mine were, and with one look, we recognized each other for what we were—powerful witches, or a powerful warlock in his case. Let me tell you, out of all the years that I have been a time-traveling, cold-case-solving witch, I have never run across my equal on the police force. Sure, I've asked other witches of the time to lend me a hand, but never one with legal authority.

The store clerk completely missed the exchange, and both the detective and I jumped back. I wasn't sure anything would happen with us just standing next to one another, but I wasn't going to chance it. Not with my powers at the surface the way they were, and apparently the detective's too.

"I was working a case just down the street when I heard the call come in," the detective said to explain his sudden appearance. Detective Cooper eyed the suspect on the ground. He didn't need to ask who took him down to know what had happened, but he did anyway. I walked him briefly through what had happened while the detective secured the suspect in handcuffs. He was clicking the last cuff on when the suspect came to. The man took one look at me over his shoulder and tried to scurry away, but his legs weren't quite working yet. The result was he sort of lolled from side to side, like a boat without oars, before losing his balance and flopping over onto his belly. That got a chuckle out of the detective. Actually, it got a chuckle out of all of us. It felt good to have the tables turned and to be back in control even if the suspect only held the power for a brief moment. Powerless wasn't a state I was comfortable with. Not even for a second.

Two uniformed cops walked in a few minutes later. If they were surprised to see the detective already there, they didn't say anything.

"You need us?" one of the police officers said by way of introduction.

"Hey, Carl," Detective Cooper replied to the officer and nodded to the second one. "I doubt this guy's buddies stuck around, but you want to take a look outside and see if you see anything? He was alone, right?" Detective Cooper turned to us for confirmation.

"I didn't see anyone else," I replied. The clerk hadn't either.

"Sure thing, boss," the officer said. Detective Cooper seemed to want to stay close to the suspect in case he fully came to and freaked out. The suspect wasn't normal—not entirely human. Of that, I was certain. But he wasn't a shifter either. Most likely, a demon or some other twisted supe taking advantage of a bad neighborhood. Ever the opportunists, those evil entities are.

Detective Cooper caught my eye while we were waiting and gave me a soft smile in return. The expression calmed me and brought me a sense of peace—more than I thought I needed at the time.

The officers came back a few minutes later. "Nothing else out there besides the usual garbage," Officer Carl said. I wasn't sure if the officer meant figuratively or literally. Given the rough crowd walking the streets, the statement could've gone either way.

"I'll get her statement," Detective Cooper said to the uniformed officers, motioning to me. "His, too," he said pointing to the clerk, whose name turned out to be Jerry.

With nothing left to do, the officers were forced to take the suspect to jail and left us to wrap the event up.

"Are you going to be okay?" I asked Jerry. He kept staring off into space, and I was searching for a way to help him.

"I'm okay. I think my heart's finally beating again." He held his hand to his chest and took a steadying breath. You could hear his anxiety on the exhale with the way the air trembled. "Maybe my sister's right. Maybe I should retire and get a little mobile home next to hers in Florida."

"That's not a bad idea," I said.

"And you can't beat the weather," Detective Cooper added. We walked Jerry out and as he went to lock the door, Detective Cooper did something that gave me the second shock of the night. He reached out and touched Jerry's hand, the key still in the store's lock. I recognized what he was doing by the look on Jerry's face. The creases from the stress that had been permanently etched on his forehead smoothed away, and peace took over the man's countenance.

"We're sure going to miss you, Jerry. But I know your sister is going to love having you close by again. Good luck with the new house in Florida," Detective Cooper said.

"Florida. It is nice down there this time a year," Jerry said.

"It's lovely every month of the year down there," I said.

"I could play golf," Jerry said.

"Every day if you want," Detective Cooper said.

"That would be nice." Jerry looked off into space again, as if he was playing a round in his head that very minute. He probably was.

"I can go ahead and call a real estate agent and get your store listed tomorrow," Detective Cooper said.

"You know a real estate agent?" Jerry asked.

"I do. She's great, and I know she'll be able to sell your store for a good price, too. Does that sound okay?"

"Yeah, that sounds good."

"How about you go ahead and call your sister and start making those travel plans tomorrow," Detective Cooper said.

"You're right, I'll do that," Jerry said. For the first time, a smile played across his face, and I felt myself smile in response. I had been adjusting people's memories for over a decade and yet I didn't think that even my technique was as smooth as Detective Cooper's here. I certainly didn't put as much thought into the alternate suggestions I often gave, but I was absolutely certain that Detective Cooper had done Jerry a favor. I had a feeling that this neighborhood was only going to get worse in the decades to come, and Jerry had worked far too long to spend his retirement years living in fear, which was exactly what would have happened if he kept working night after night in a convenience store that was regularly robbed. I shuddered at the thought of might have happened if I hadn't been in the store that night. Would the suspect have shot Jerry when he froze? I had the sickening feeling that he would have.

We saw Jerry to his apartment, which was around the block. And I saw that was right; while his apartment still looked nice with freshly swept steps, a welcome mat, and potted petunias on the porch, his neighbor's porch was crumbling, and the doorframe looked like it had been kicked in on more than one occasion given the splintered wood and dented door.

"Coffee?" Detective Cooper said to me once Jerry was tucked safely inside his home.

"I'd love a cup," I replied. I had no idea if Penny was still inside the billiard hall, but right at that moment, I wanted to talk to Detective Cooper more.

His car was parked further down the street. The grille said Chevrolet, the color was black, and I had a feeling it went fast. I thought the detective was either really trusting or really lucky to park such a nice-looking car in this suburb and still have it be there when he got back to it. That was until I saw how the average person would see it—as a rusted-out car missing two tires. Detective Cooper had used magic, most likely a charm or ward, to disguise his ride. It was smart and a bit complicated to pull off, which only upped my esteem for the detective.

He walked me to the car and held the door open for me while I ducked inside. My hand automatically reached over my shoulder to grab my seatbelt, only to come up empty. I felt like such a rebel riding in a car without a seatbelt and felt the need to mutter a bit of my own charm—a safety one—as an added protection.

Neither the detective nor I said anything while he got behind the wheel and pulled away from the curb. I didn't ask where we were going, and as long as the coffee was somewhat decent, I didn't really care.

"That was ..." Detective Cooper's words trailed off as we put the slum behind us.

"Something," I said, filling in the blank for him.

"I've never met someone like you, or someone like me, I guess," he said.

"Yeah, me neither. Well, besides my mom," I answered honestly. I knew plenty of powerful witches, but none of them possessed the same electrifying skills as I did.

"You're right. My mom had the same gift," Detective Cooper said. We were both silent for a minute. Then he said, "I've never seen you around here before."

I was pretty sure that was the detective's way of asking

me what I was doing down in Harlem late at night. But I wasn't going to answer that question, not yet. Instead, I replied, "That's because I'm not from around here."

"Oh yeah?"

"Yeah, Michigan born and raised," I replied, explaining the where I was from, but obviously not the when.

"That explains the accent," Detective Cooper said.

"Excuse me? Accent? Hate to break it to you, buddy, but you're the one that talks funny. You're New Yorker through and through."

"And proud of it," he said.

Detective Cooper pulled into a twenty-four-hour donut shop. The irony of a cop choosing a donut shop was just the comedic relief my night needed. That, and I could have surely used a chocolate glazed donut. Maybe two.

"BUSINESS OR PLEASURE?" Detective Cooper asked me after we selected our donuts and sat in a booth across from one another. With our donuts and coffee in front of us, I would have loved to bypass the detective's question and dig right in, but I didn't. I was polite like that.

"Business," I said, and *then* I took a bite of my donut. I didn't say it had to be a lengthy response.

Part of the reason that I'm good at my job is I'm usually pretty good at picking apart a person's character. I liked Detective Cooper. He had good energy and it wasn't just because he was a cop with magical talents. Maybe there was something in that zap we shared, but I trusted him. Even so, the Agency had rules. I couldn't go spilling everything to him —even if I wanted to, but that didn't mean we couldn't work together.

"Like you, Detective—"

"Call me Michael," he said, interrupting me.

"Okay, like you, Michael, I'm working a case. A private one," I added before he could ask. "A young witch named Irene has gone missing. It's been almost four days now. Her best friend, Penny, works the cosmetics counter at Macy's. I've talked to her once and I wanted to talk to her again. I tracked Penny to the billiard hall and I was waiting for her to leave so I could question her when the robbery took place at the convenience store."

"I know," Michael said.

"You know?" I shook my head incredulously. "What do you mean, you know?"

"Well, I saw you. I was inside the hall looking for someone when you caught my eye."

"You saw me? I didn't see you." I suddenly was more annoyed than I should have been. I was so focused on completing my mission and avoiding the shifters' detection that I hadn't looked out for normal human beings ... well, normal enough. It was a rookie mistake. I knew better.

Michael seemed to read me like I had just read him and came to the same conclusion. And that he could trust me. He took a drink of his coffee and then said, "Your case is similar to mine. A young witch goes missing and no one has seen her since. The only lead I have is a potential boyfriend, a shifter named Rick Canali, who I tracked to the billiard hall as well."

"When did your girl go missing?" I asked.

"Friday, although Melody's foster parents just notified us on Monday."

"Why did they wait so long?" I couldn't get over how many parents seemed to just not care when their kids went missing.

"She has a history of running away. If I hadn't known she was a witch and her potential boyfriend a shifter? I wouldn't have thought anything of it either."

"You know her." I said it as a statement not a question.

"It's not the first time I've tracked her down. The first time I caught up with her, she threw out such a forceful orb shield that it about knocked me unconscious."

"Wow," I said, raising my eyebrows.

"I know. Melody's power is something else, which is why I offered to help her—not with her foster parents; they would never understand. They're the most mundane individuals in the history of mankind—but to introduce her to a coven in the area. A group of good witches that could train her and give her a sense of family."

"It didn't work out?" I asked.

Michael shook his head. "Obviously not."

We both ate our donuts and sat lost in our own thoughts for a few moments.

"Something big is going on in the Manhattan supernatural community. I've felt it building for months, but I can't crack it. These missing young witches are just the tip of it."

I wanted to argue with the detective, but I had a sinking suspicion that he was right.

"I'll make you a deal. I'll tell you everything that I can about this case as long as you do the same," I offered.

Michael didn't even hesitate. He held out his hand. "Deal," he said before dropping it and smirking. "Maybe we shouldn't shake on it?"

"Yeah, let's forget the handshake," I said.

"What's your next move?" the detective asked me.

"I'm working undercover as a housekeeper for Irene's parents."

"They don't know that you're a ..."

"They don't know anything. Their biggest concern is what the neighbors think." I took a sip of my coffee. "I still need to talk to Penny." That reminded me of something else. "Did you try scrying for Melody?"

"No go." Michael looked slightly embarrassed. "Scrying isn't really my strong suit. I tried, but I was blocked." The detective shook his head.

"It's not just you. It happened to me too. Someone's cloaking these girls' location."

"I didn't even think of that. I just thought ... well, like I said, scrying doesn't usually work well for me. I'm a more hands-on search kind of guy."

"I have an idea. What if we try to locate them together? Two witches are more powerful than one," I said.

"I'm game to try." Michael eyed the donut shop. "Not sure this is really the best spot," he said.

"No, I agree, plus I have to get back." I wasn't sure I could talk my way out of being out of the house in the middle of the night. I'd be erasing the Hendrickses' memories if they caught me for sure. "What's your schedule look like tomorrow morning?"

"I can make whatever work."

"Okay, the Hendrickses are usually out of the house by ten o'clock. Want to meet up after then?"

"Sure. I'll wait for you downstairs."

"Perfect."

CHAPTER 10

*M*ichael gave me a ride back to the apartment and he didn't even raise an eyebrow when I told him to park one street over so I could sneak in the back. There was something to be said for working with another professional that got you. I found them to be few and far between. My best friend, Lexi, is the only other one that comes to mind. I managed to sneak back into my room unnoticed and let out a sigh of relief. Day four was officially breaking, which meant I had to work overtime to solve this case. It didn't matter what year I was in, time always seemed to move faster when I didn't want it to. Instead of getting answers, my run-in with the detective gave me more questions. Questions I didn't know I'd have to time to answer.

The sun wasn't even fully up when I heard a commotion outside my bedroom door in the kitchen. Cupboards were being slammed, drawers forcibly jarred open by the sound of the silverware clanging about, and Mr. Hendricks was mumbling to himself. I hadn't even managed an hour of shut-eye, but that was going to have to cut it. I needed to get out there stat and find out what was going on.

"Mary, make Mrs. Hendricks her special tea," Mr. Hendricks instructed me as he raced past the kitchen. I walked through the kitchen and watched as he unbuttoned his shirt sleeves and rolled them up. Mr. Hendricks walked to the front door, then turned and walked back down the hall, stopping at a closet and opening it. His head disappeared for a moment and when it reappeared, he was tugging luggage out with it. He took the suitcase into the master bedroom and returned empty handed, looking about the apartment, before turning once more and heading further down the hall, this time into Irene's bedroom. Within another minute, he was back with another suitcase.

"I'm sorry, Mr. Hendricks?" I said.

The man quit walking up the hallway and looked at me.

"You'd like me to make Mrs. Hendricks some tea?"

"That's right. Mary's not here. She puts a tonic in Madeline's tea when her nerves are troubling her. It's somewhere in the kitchen," Mr. Hendricks said, talking with his hands. He then vanished back into the master bedroom.

"Okay, tea with tonic, coming right up," I said to myself.

"And turn off the phone's ringer. I don't want it disturbing Madeline while she tries to gets some rest," he poked his head out of the bedroom to add.

"Tea and phone ringer. You got it."

I searched the kitchen for anything that might resemble tonic, not even sure what I was looking for. But then I remembered the brown bottles with the little rubber stoppers Mary had lined up on her own kitchen counter. I found just that in an upper side cupboard. It was next to the brandy and the cooking sherry. I twisted off the stopper and smelled the light-colored liquid inside. It was slightly floral and sweet smelling, but I had no idea what it was.

"Mr. Hendricks, is this it?" I said taking the bottle to the living room. Mr. Hendricks was bringing more luggage out, clothes sticking out of the sides from the wardrobe being tossed in and the suitcase closed without care.

"Does it look like a tonic?" he asked in return without looking up. He seemed to be analyzing the luggage. Perhaps he was wondering if he had packed everything?

"Yes, I suppose it does."

"Then what is the question?" he replied, still not looking up.

"How much do I put in?"

"I don't know. That's your job. I don't ask you what the weight of gold is, or where magnesium is on the periodic table of elements, and you don't ask me about kitchen work."

I bit my tongue and walked back to the kitchen. Chances were good that this was the tonic Mary put in Mrs. Hendricks' tea, but it could also be perfume given how sweet the mixture smelled. I could always call Mary and check with her. Or I could just guess and do things my way. I went with option number three and put a splash of brandy in the tea, knowing for a fact that would calm the missus' nerves as good as any tonic.

I delivered the tea along with some buttered toast. After all, you shouldn't drink on an empty stomach. The curtains were drawn in the master bedroom, dimming the morning sunlight. Like the guest room, the carpet here was pink, as were the bedspread and curtains. There wasn't a touch of masculinity in the Hendrickses' home decor. A glass and gold-rimmed vanity filled with perfume bottles and facial creams was pushed against the wall, in front of the bed. The vanity was a twin to the one in Irene's bedroom, only this one was super-sized.

Mrs. Hendricks sat up and leaned forward for me to stack her pillows behind her back. A velvet robe was tied across her slim waist. Her hair was pinned up and her lashes were

BETTER WITCH NEXT TIME

on, leaving me to question just how nerved up the lady of the house was.

"Is it my special tea?" Mrs. Hendricks asked, taking the saucer from my hands. I placed a similar plate with the toast on it on her bedside table.

"It's my special tea. I'm sure you'll enjoy it."

She put the dainty cup to her lips and took a tentative sip. Her eyes closed in appreciation. I took that as a good sign.

I left Mrs. Hendricks to her breakfast and went in search of Mr. Hendricks to see what he was up to, or more like, where he was off to.

The man was still pacing the hallway, opening this closet and that one, and piling items into the suitcase.

"Can I assist you with anything else?" I asked Mr. Hendricks, referencing the luggage before him.

"I'm taking Mrs. Hendricks to the Catskills. Some mountain air will serve her well," he said, taking a raincoat out of the closet and cramming it into the already full suitcase.

"You're leaving?"

"I don't know why I let Mrs. Hendricks talk me into spending the summer in the city. We never spend the summer here and look at what good that got us. No, I need to get her out of here. A change of scenery will do her a world of good."

"But what about Irene?"

"Why, what have you heard about her?" Mr. Hendricks stopped moving and stared at me. His eyes were suddenly cold.

"Nothing, I just thought you might want to stay around in town in case she turned up."

"And let it ruin her mother's health in the meantime? No, Irene is a grown woman. She's made her choices. Let her live with them."

I didn't know how to respond to that, which was why I asked him when they would be back instead.

Mr. Hendricks answered my question by saying, "You're free to go."

"Excuse me?"

"Your services are no longer needed. I'm sure Mary will be able to return to work once we are back in town."

I hadn't been expecting that. I tried to think quickly on my feet for a reason for me to stay. "If you're certain?"

"Of course I'm certain. And I don't appreciate you questioning my judgment like this," Mr. Hendricks snapped at me.

At that moment, the Hendrickses' cat, George, decided to make his presence known with a rather heartfelt meow. "And what about George? Will you be taking him with you?" I asked.

Mr. Hendricks looked down at the cat. "Where in the devil did he come from?"

"He's your cat."

"Well, I never saw the animal before. Take him with you." I looked down at George who looked back up at me and appeared to shrug his shoulders. I knew there was no point in arguing since Mr. Hendricks would just get even more snippy. Just like I knew that if I still wanted to stay there, all I had to do was climb back up the fire escape after they left or walk right in the front door. After all, locks were no problem for me to open.

"You can't get rid of the cat," Mrs. Hendricks said from behind us. I hadn't even heard her walk up the hallway.

"Excuse me?" Mr. Hendricks asked.

"Jillian loves that cat," Mrs. Hendricks said in a matter-of-fact tone.

"Mrs. Morgan?" Mr. Hendricks sounded incredulous.

"Yes! And James too. You can't get rid of George. After

James and Irene are married, that cat is his. Then you will be rid of it. Until then, the cat stays, as does Anna.

"Madeline, you can't seriously think—"

"Seriously think what? That James will marry Irene? Of course I think it. Why in the heavens wouldn't I?"

"Because ... nothing." Mr. Hendricks glowered, but he didn't dare say another word. Not with Mrs. Hendricks present. No, he waited until she was out of earshot before saying, "Fine, you can stay, but don't expect your full salary!" His finger punctuated the air.

"Of course not, sir," I said dryly before clearing my throat and putting on a proper attitude.

Mr. Hendricks gave me the eye, but only said, "Now fetch Henry. I need him to come get these bags and call for my car."

I WALKED OUT OF THE HENDRICKSES' building and found Michael. He was chatting up the old man at the newspaper stand, the one I had given the tonic to the day before. And by the way they were chatting, it seemed like they knew one another.

"Hi, guys," I said, interrupting their conversation.

"Officially off duty?" Michael asked me, taking in my appearance. Not knowing where we were going, I opted to change back into the dress I had traveled back in time with. I would rather be dressed up for an occasion versus dressed down. And no, the fact that the detective was an attractive man had nothing to do with my wardrobe choice. Or at least, that was what I was telling myself.

"Permanently," I replied.

The detective raised his eyebrows.

"You ready to go and I'll fill you in?" I asked.

"Hang on, I was just getting The Daily here from Sid."

"That's right, I should have known when you gave me that tonic, miss," Sid replied.

I wasn't really following, but that didn't stop me from saying, "Oh, did it work?"

"Like a dream. Thanks, sweetheart," Sid lifted his newsboy cap to me in acknowledgement. Then he disappeared from sight, bending over to retrieve something for Michael. When he stood, I saw that it was in fact a newspaper. Unlike the other newspapers that were on display, this one was rolled up so that the front page was hidden, and the paper was tied shut with a piece of brown twine. Michael gave Sid a dime and then motioned for me to follow him down the sidewalk. While we walked, Michael untied the string and read the front page. The paper looked completely ordinary in size and layout. It wasn't until you took a moment to read the headlines that you noticed it was different.

"Another missing teen witch. Mundane parents clueless," and "Werewolf found dead. Suspect at large," dominated the front page.

"A supernatural newspaper?" I asked.

"You haven't heard of The Daily? You are from the Midwest, aren't you?" Michael joked.

"That makes Sid what?" I said, thinking back to the source. I didn't pick up the shifter vibe from him. If he had been a witch, he could have made his own tonic. He definitely wasn't dead or a demon. "Warlock, shifter, ghost?" I said for clarification.

"Oh, no. Sid is a bit eccentric, but he's completely normal."

That's a relief. I was beginning to think my supernatural senses had stayed in the future.

I looked over at the paper. I suppose it should be no surprise that a city of this size had its own supernatural news network. Just what would they think of next?

"It just doesn't make sense. Usually the apex predators

stick to their own turf," Michael said, reading an article tucked away on page two. "What has them on the move and who's killing them?" he said mostly to himself.

He folded up the newspaper and tucked it under his arm. "There's someone that I want to talk to. Do you mind taking a drive with me?"

"No, not at all. Did you still want to try to scry for the girls?"

"I have an idea on that front too. I'm hoping my source can help us out."

"Okay, and what about Penny? She's the one I was waiting on last night."

"I remembered you saying that, and I've tracked her down."

"You did?" I stopped walking in surprise.

"Don't act so shocked, it's my job."

"No, it's just ... I haven't been able to." I tried not to sound annoyed. In a matter of hours, Michael had tracked down Penny's residence, and I had been forced to stake out a billiard hall in the ghetto. Of course, if I hadn't been there I wouldn't have bumped into the detective here. Now I wasn't sure what emotion to go with.

"Turns out when you have a badge, people talk," Michael said, walking once more.

I made a mental note to add "request badge" at our next agency debriefing session. "I suppose that's true," I said catching up.

"It is. I remembered you saying she worked at the makeup counter at Macy's. I called the human resources department there, gave them my credentials, and got her address. I thought we could go there afterwards."

MICHAEL NAVIGATED us out of the city, and before I knew it, we were headed south on I-95. "So the Hendrickses let you go?" he asked.

"Technically, they don't need me or any housekeeper at the moment because Mr. Hendricks took his wife to the Catskills. Apparently, the stress of Irene's disappearance has finally caught up with her, or maybe the stress of having to act as if everything is perfectly normal has. Anyway, he packed up their luggage and they took off about thirty minutes before you got there. But I'm not totally canned."

"No?"

"No, I've been demoted to cat sitter. Although I like to think of it as a promotion."

"How's that?"

"I'd rather care for George the cat then the Hendricks any day of the week."

"They're that bad, huh?"

"They're something else, that's for sure."

"Did Mr. Hendricks say where in the Catskills they were headed?"

"No, and I didn't even think to ask. I imagine he'll come back to the city though. I have a feeling the man isn't one for taking vacations."

"No, you're probably right. Most likely, they have a standing resort that they go to every summer. I'm sure he will get settled and then return."

"So where are we headed?" I asked.

"My sister's," Michael looked in his rearview mirror before changing lanes.

"Your sister is your source?" I asked.

"No, my grandmother is my source. She lives with my sister and her family."

"Oh, well, why don't we just call her?"

"You'll see," the detective replied, leaving it at that.

CHAPTER 11

*O*ver an hour later, the detective's car was bumping down a country road. The setting reminded me an awful lot like home, especially when the farmhouse came into view, complete with the wide front porch and large maple tree out front. The tree cast the house in shade, which I knew was appreciated this time of year. The dust hadn't even settled around the car after we pulled in the driveway and parked when a gaggle of kids came running out the front door and down the steps to greet us. Three large dogs followed in their footsteps, barking.

"Uncle Michael! Uncle Michael!" the collection of kids shouted. All of them were quite young, and I dare say that the oldest was yet ten. With bare feet and big smiles, they were a bundle-of-energy.

"Even if my sister did have a phone, you'd be hard-pressed to have a conversation with these youngsters around," Michael joked. We got out of the car and I looked up and saw a woman standing on the front porch. She was wearing a white dress with a yellow floral print and drying her hands on an apron. Michael was busy high-fiving and hugging his niece and nephews, even giving the dogs some love, scratching their ears.

"Is everything okay?" the woman asked with concern in her eyes as we approached. As we got closer, I could tell that she was his sister. She had the same eyes as her brother. They could look right through you and flesh out the truth. The kids took off chasing one another around the front yard, the dogs in close pursuit, before they all scrambled back up the porch and disappeared inside the house.

Michael didn't answer his sister's question and instead he said, "This is Vee. She's helping me work a case. Is Gran awake?"

"Are you serious? You can't take a nap in this household." The sound of screaming reached us outside. It was hard to say if it was laughter-induced or pain-inflicted. Seeing as the detective's sister didn't move, I assumed it was the former. "Gran's around back, hanging up the wash. I'm Karen by the way," she said extending her hand for me to shake, which I did, but unlike when I shook her brother's hand, nothing remarkable happened. "This visit have anything to do with those apex killings?" Karen asked steadily.

Michael looked surprised at his sister. "You heard about those?"

"Sam told me about them. He said some shifters were talking about it in Philly."

"Philly? I guess I'm not the only person who's noticed. Sam around?" Michael asked.

"No, he's back to working days. Says it's as boring as can be, but I'm not going to lie, I like having him home at night."

"I'm sure you do. Maybe I'll try to call him at work. See what else he's heard," Michael replied.

"You do that. Sam said everyone's getting jittery, and I don't think it's just because of the full moon this month," Karen said.

"No, I don't think so either." Michael looked over his shoulder at me. Personally, I didn't know what to think. I wasn't here to solve some shifter mystery, I just needed to find Irene, and fast. Time was running out.

"Stop back inside after you're done talking to Gran, you hear?" Karen said, turning to walk to the door.

"You got it," Michael replied.

"Who's Sam?" I asked as we walked around the side of the house.

"My brother-in-law. He's PD in Philly."

"Oh? I didn't know we were close." Had we already crossed into Pennsylvania?

"It's about forty minutes away. Sam doesn't mind the commute. Says the country soothes him."

"And you?" I asked.

"I'd take the city any day," Michael said. "The urban jungle soothes me."

As we came around back, I saw Michael's grandmother. Her pure white hair flowed loosely down her back, blowing like the white sheets hanging on the line. Her face was as translucent and wrinkled as a piece of used tissue paper. Her eyes were clear and blue as a pool of cool water.

"I knew you were coming. I just didn't know when you would get here," she said, closing the distance and giving her grandson a hug.

She then turned to me. "I'm Edith," she said, holding me at arm's length and studying me. "And you, miss ... you're not from around here, are you?" she said with a wink and gave me a hug as well.

I answered her question with a smile and said, "It's lovely to meet you."

Edith went back to hanging up the pile of laundry in the basket at her feet. Michael stepped in and took the wooden clips from his grandmother to finish the task. "

Always such a good boy," she said, patting his hand.

The detective hung up another white sheet and a few shirts. The third time he reached up, his shirt came untucked, revealing the piece he kept holstered in the small of his back, proving that he was as much detective as he was witch.

"What's troubling you, dear? Unless you're just here to do the laundry. Heaven knows we have plenty of it," Edith said. Kids bumbled out the back door and ran toward a pond on the far side of the property. I couldn't see them once they passed through a line of apple trees, but I heard several splashes, followed by squalls of laughter and the squawking of ducks as they made a hasty retreat.

"Something is going on in the supernatural community. Shifters are being killed. Witches are missing." Michael shook his head. "I can't help but think they're all connected, and it's happened before. I remember you telling me about the shifter war years ago."

"Indeed, that was a dark time for the supernatural community. You think it's starting again?" Edith looked off into the distance as if she was trying to see for herself what was unfolding. She nodded solemnly.

"Tell me about the shifters," Edith said.

"It's been in the paper. Apex predators are turning up dead," Michael said.

"Wolves and panthers?" Edith asked.

"Tigers too," Michael said.

I sucked in a breath. I hadn't heard any of this. Weretigers were the rarest shifter of all. As far as I knew, they stayed out of pack politics, preferring to be lone rangers. Besides that fact, many considered them to be the fiercest shifter of all. Attacking them was the equivalent of a suicide mission.

"And the witches?" Edith asked.

"That's where Vee comes in here. She was tracking a missing teen witch. The same as me. Both of our girls have disappeared without a trace. They're not weak either," he said, looking to me for confirmation.

"No, they're not," I said thinking of Archie's comments about Irene's psychic and fire power.

"You think the shifters are using them as pawns?" Edith asked.

The detective nodded. "It's an idea I've been tossing around."

My mouth dropped open. I hadn't even considered the possibility, but I had to admit that the theory held some weight.

"Right now it's just a guess. Until we can find these girls, we won't know one way or the other," he added.

"You tried to scry?" Edith asked.

"Both of us have. No luck. Someone supernatural is cloaking them. I was hoping you could help us see them," Michael said.

The kids continued to splash and shriek in the water, even louder now as the dogs jumped in the pond with them.

"Not here, that's for sure. Come, take a walk with me." Edith grabbed the cane that was perched against the clothes-line pole and motioned with her head for us to follow her. While I was happy that I had worn a dress for the occasion, I hadn't necessarily planned on going for any hikes. Thankfully, I had opted to wear my black ballet flats versus the heels. Maybe I had a little psychic power of my own.

Edith took us down a narrow dirt path that was only the width of our two feet. With her as the leader, our pace was slow, but our progress was steady as we walked around the outside of the pond and alongside the planted crop fields to a patch of woods located at the back of the property. Eventually the noise from shrieking children and barking dogs grew quieter the further we walked out. Edith wound us into the woods with nothing more than nature surrounding us.

Sunlight filtered down through the full-leaf trees and birds chirped all around us.

But as we walked on, even they seemed to quiet down. None of us spoke as we continued on in a single-file line. Then the woods opened into a small meadow. It was less than an acre but full of peace and tranquility. The ground was full of purple and blue wildflowers. White butterflies fluttered about, and grasshoppers seemed to pop up and fly a few feet every time we took a step. Bumble bees buzzed, and I caught Michael's eye as he resisted the urge to swat at one, knowing how much of a mistake that would be.

"I think I've spent too much time beating the pavement," he whispered to me.

"We should change that," I said before I could stop myself. In my head, a vision played out with Michael and I going camping. How fun would that be? To get the city boy reacquainted with nature. I stopped the thought at that, not wanting to play out any fantasy that could never be a reality. It was one thing to think of the detective as an attractive man and appreciate his help with this case, and quite another to think that I would ever see him again after my time here was up. Furthermore, I reminded myself of how charming men could seem at first, and how utterly annoying they became after you got to know them. Flashes of Andrew crying on my front porch came to mind. I really hoped I wouldn't see that man again. Thinking of Andrew was enough to squash any romantic feelings I had subconsciously been entertaining for Detective Cooper, which was how I was going to refer to him from now on. I didn't care if he wanted me to call him Michael or not, I was going to stick with professional titles from here on out. If only he could refer to me as Agent Vee. Of course, the agent title would only lead to more questions, such as what agency I worked for, which was a no go.

In the center of the meadow was a small pool not more

than four feet in diameter. From the middle of it, pristine spring water bubbled up. It was just enough to disrupt the surface and push the water out in little waves, where it gently wetted the surrounding rocks. I peered into the pool but only saw the darkness, rendering me unable to gauge how deep the spring went. Edith handed Michael, wait ... I mean Detective Cooper, her cane and slowly sank to her knees so that her palms were pressed on the soil and her body leaned over the pool of water. Softly, she began to chant. The words were in a foreign tongue; perhaps it was Latin with its heavy reliance on vowels. The rhythm of the words sounded familiar, but the meaning was lost on me. The spring began to bubble more in response to her words. Edith sat back on her heels and raised her hands up to shoulder level with her palms outstretched to the sun, eyes closed. She continued her chant as the water swirled and bubbled before her and then the fog rose up, only this time, it was caused by Edith. She was commanding the fog to show us what it had been hiding. Detective Cooper stood at my side as the soft images came into focus. Irene, Melody, and a third girl, one who I had never seen before, were all being held captive together. I tried to make out the details, like the thick rope that bound their wrists and the packed dirt floor under their feet, but it was hard to make out any other specifics in the darkness. Edith waved her hand in front of the fog, like a person cleaning a window, and the image became clearer.

The image zoomed in closer, and the looks on the girls' faces varied. Irene looked alert as if she was waiting for someone to attack. Melody was seething. It was clear that both of these girls were ready to fight. The third girl stared at the floor as tears streamed down her cheeks, defeated.

"Where are they?" I whispered.

Detective Cooper shook his head. "I don't know."

Then in an instant, a big gust of wind came and tore

through the field, taking the fog and scattering it up to the heavens. The wind hit Edith in the chest, knocking her backwards until she was flat on her back on the ground. The water from the spring shot into the sky like a water jet. The drops came raining down on us with the force of a summer thunderstorm. Detective Cooper bent down to scoop Edith under her arms and lift her up. The winds whipped through the meadow as we backed up and sought shelter in the enclave of the trees. Dark clouds blotted out the sun like a full eclipse. Lightning struck the ground. Rain pelted all around us. I brought my forearm across my face to block the stinging drops. I held my breath for an instant before my witch reflexes kicked in. This was a magical onslaught, and it would take one to stop it.

Detective Cooper must have realized the same thing at that instant, as his hand clasped with mine and together we created our own electrical light show. You know what they say, fight fire with fire, and that's exactly what we were doing, sending lightning bolts into the sky and frying the source of the attack.

The sky lit up like an explosion. There was enough current in the air to charge all of Manhattan. My hair stood on end. The ground began to hum. If we weren't careful, we would short circuit ourselves and then some.

The winds picked up. The rain blew sideways. Edith rocked back on her heels.

We needed a different approach.

"Protection spell!" I hollered over the howling winds.

"For every witch, in every hour, send us now the greatest power," Detective Cooper commanded.

"Rid all evil from this space. Grant us your amazing grace!" the three of us finished together. A white light shot forth from the center of the spring. Like a beacon of hope, it pierced the storm and destroyed the spell that was wreaking havoc on our peaceful meadow.

When it was over, Michael (yes, I was back to referring to him as Michael) had his arm wrapped protectively over his grandmother's shoulder, his other hand clasped fiercely with mine. He and I looked at one another, unsure what to make of any of it. I let go of his hand and smoothed out my dress, staring at the ground. The detective wrapped his grandmother in a full embrace from the side and gave her a kiss on the top of her head.

"Well, you can definitely say trouble is brewing," Edith said with a chuckle. "You kids have your work cut out for you," she said, her eyes now getting serious.

"Who's the third girl?" I asked Michael.

"I don't know. I only know of two missing witches, but New York City is a big place and who's to say that's where she's from?"

"We have to find them," I said.

"Did you get a feeling for where they were located?" Michael asked his grandmother.

"I'm not sure. They're isolated. Somewhere by water? I'm not sure if that's right." Edith wrung her hands. "I'm just not as powerful as I used to be." Disappointment seemed to hitch onto her words.

"You're more powerful than we are," I said motioning to Michael and me. "I never even thought to use the fog. I just tried getting rid of it," I said to make my point.

"But you're stronger together. Never forget that," Edith shook her finger at us. I nodded. That was Witchcraft 101. Witches are always stronger when they work together, which was why I asked Michael to scry with me to find the girls.

"I'm sorry, kids, but I think I need a rest. Let's go back to the house and see if Karen has lunch ready."

"Do you want me to help you back?" Michael asked Edith.

"I said that I needed a rest, not that I was an invalid," she said with a laugh. "Come on, let's get going."

Karen was surveying the backyard, waiting for us to emerge. When she spotted us break through the tree line, she couldn't keep herself from running across the field toward us.

"My word, what on earth has happened to you guys?"

I self-consciously brushed my hand through my hair, which was actually almost dry, and looked down at my dress, which unfortunately wasn't. Neither were my shoes, the backs of which were digging into my heels, and I knew I would have some pretty impressive blisters in a few hour's time.

"Come now, let me get you some dry clothes and some-thing to eat," she said to all of us. Thankfully, the kids were still being crazy outside, so the four of us were able to go inside and get cleaned up in relative peace and quiet.

"Here, I hope this is okay," Karen said handing me a freshly laundered dress cut in the similar fashion and fabric as the one she was wearing.

"This is wonderful, thank you so much." I took the folded dress from Karen. She added a towel to the top of the dress and pointed me in the direction of the bathroom for me to get cleaned up. I was beyond grateful to have dry clothes to put on and to see Karen preparing an amazing farm-fresh lunch—even the smell of the fried chicken didn't bother me.

The grease was sizzling and popping while Karen manned the skillet on the stove when I emerged. The stovetop resembled one that I was more familiar with, with only four burners and one oven door. The ironic thing was, she could have used the larger oven with a family her size, while the Hendrickses could have done well with this smaller version.

"Some storm this afternoon, huh?" she said, using a pair of metal tongs to flip the pieces of chicken over in the pan.

"Could you see it from here?" I asked.

"Nope, just a feeling I had," she said with a knowing look. I nodded. Then Michael joined us in the kitchen, his wet trousers and dress shirt hung over his arm. "Tell Sam thanks for the clothes. I appreciate it. Here," he said picking up my damp dress off the back of the kitchen chair. "Why don't I go hang our stuff up outside on the line?"

"Yeah, good thinking. I'll come with you."

We walked outside together, neither one of us speaking until we were at the clothesline.

"Are you okay?" Michael asked me, picking up a wooden clothespin and hanging my dress on the line for me.

"Yeah, you?" I asked.

"I'm good."

"How are we going to find these girls? Do you really think the shifters can lead us to them?"

"It's the best lead we have. I'm going to call the station and see if I can get a beat on the third girl."

"Did you see her face? Michael, we don't have a lot of time."

"I know we don't."

"If it's not the shifters—" I didn't get to finish my sentence.

"Then we'll find out who."

I didn't have the heart to tell the detective that no one ever found out the truth.

Karen began bringing lunch outside and eyed us across the yard. We put our conversation on pause to join her and set the table. Lemonade, fried chicken, corn on the cob, macaroni salad, watermelon, fresh veggies with dip—Karen had pulled out all the stops. The adults chose to sit at the picnic table while the kids ran around the yard with their fried chicken, hair still damp from their dip in the pond, and the dogs barking and jumping after them, hoping to snag a piece of meat for themselves.

"You, Karen, are an amazing cook," I said, eyeing the platter of fried-to-perfection chicken in front of me. If there was ever any dish to tempt a vegetarian, that was it.

"Sorry, I didn't know you didn't eat meat," Karen replied.

"Oh, that's all right, how would you? Plus, there's plenty for me to eat. This is wonderful, really. "

"Why, thank you. I learned from the best," Karen said, nodding to Edith who was sitting on the bench next to her.

As enjoyable as lunch had been, I knew Michael was just as anxious as I was to get back to the city and track down the girls. If we never found them, the images of them bound together would haunt me forever.

Karen looked around to make sure the kids were all out of earshot and not paying attention before she asked, "What did you guys find out?"

Michael held up three fingers. "Three girls, all being held together. Witches, I'm assuming."

"Shifters?" Karen asked.

"We still don't know," I said.

Edith sat across from me, her face twisted in a scowl. I knew it was just as frustrating to her as it was to us that the person or persons behind these disappearances were still a mystery.

"Peter!" Edith hollered across the yard to a young boy who was running with his dog. "Go upstairs in my room and fetch me my book." Edith left it at that, and Peter apparently knew exactly which book she meant since he did just as he was told.

"There's a spell you can try. Together—of course. Witches are always stronger together. If you need more power you can always ask another to chime in, but I think the two of you can manage it on your own," Edith said with a wink.

Peter brought the book to the table and ran off just as quickly as he had come. The book was soft black leather. The symbol of an eye had been embossed on the cover, raising the edges up, along with the initials E. C. in an old English script. I peered over Michael's shoulder and attempted to read Edith's book of shadows. Michael flipped through the book waiting for Edith to tell him where to stop. The pages were thick, white parchment, some of the edges torn, along with smudges here and there. Black wax had dripped onto the page that she pointed to. The page didn't have a title at the top, not like what you find nowadays in commercial spell books, only a list of ingredients, the amounts scratched out and rewritten two or three times, along with the incantation and notes scrawled in the margin. "Best under full moon," I read out loud. That was a given. Almost all spells worked best under the full moon. Under that she had written "or when waning to decrease enemy power."

"A weakening spell?" I asked.

"And a good one too. It'll make them nervous. Increase their fears and doubts."

"A crack in their shield should be all we need," Michael said mostly to himself as he read over the spell.

He was right. If we could weaken the enemies' hold, we should be able to find out exactly where they were holding the girls and then attack before they were able to strengthen their resolve.

"Bingo," Edith said.

I couldn't help but wish Edith was a few decades younger and up to fighting this battle. I had a feeling she would be one heck of a spitfire in a shifter fight.

At that moment, Karen sprang from the picnic table and shot her arms out in front of her, fingers sprawled out, her energy directed toward the large maple in the backyard, where one of her kids, a little boy, was falling head first toward the ground. But instead of barreling into the dirt, his body came to a screeching halt. While he was temporarily suspended in the air, Karen walked across the yard, lecturing the whole way. "Calvin Thomas, how many times do I have to tell you not to climb trees? You're going to break your neck!"

I had a feeling the little boy would've run away from his mom if he hadn't been frozen in midair. She walked up to him, plucked him from suspension, and set him on his feet. At that, he did take off running, just in case his mother decided to give him a swat on the butt.

"I swear, these kids," Karen said more to herself than anyone else.

"Your sister can suspend objects?" I asked out of the corner of my mouth.

"Oh yeah. She took freeze tag to a whole new level when we were kids."

"Oh my goodness, I bet."

"Fortunately for us, it only lasts a minute."

Calvin's tumble from the tree officially ended our lunch, and we quickly helped clean up and said our goodbyes after that.

"Do you want to work Edith's spell first or go and see if Penny's home?" Michael asked me as we rolled back onto the country road.

I had just asked myself the same question.

"How about we get the supplies we need, go see if Penny's home, and then work the spell if we need to." I was hopeful Penny knew more than she had led me to believe and I'd be able to coerce it out of her.

CHAPTER 12

*T*he ingredients looked pretty simple—a few candles, frankincense, and sea salt. If I was back at home, I could order the whole entire lot off of Amazon or drive into town to our own curios shop. It wasn't hard to find new age items in the modern world.

"How hard is this to come by?" I asked, turning the book to Michael's direction.

"What do you mean, like in New York or...?"

"No I meant like—" Oops. I had almost said in nineteen fifty-eight. What in the world was I thinking? That's what you get for getting too comfortable with someone. Your guard goes down and secrets slip out. I was going to have to be more careful. I cleared my throat. "No, I meant like from your apartment. Isn't that where you'd like to work the spell?" I said, quickly improvising.

"Oh ... sure. We can work it back at my place, that's fine. There's a shop just a bit out of the way where we can get everything, too."

"There is?" I guess I shouldn't be too surprised, seeing as the supernatural community here did have their own newspaper. A supernatural supply shop was nothing compared to that.

"Yes, there is. We just need to head down to Radio Alley."

"Radio what?" I looked at Michael not following.

"You haven't heard of Radio Alley either?"

"No." I said, my voice wavering a bit. "Do they have a lot of radios there?"

"Well, they used to. Remember how popular radios were a few years ago?"

I nodded. Television was old technology in my time, but its popularity was really starting to soar in the late fifties.

"Well, when all you had was your radio and it broke, you had to go from one appliance store to the next to find the right parts. With so many radios and so many people here in New York City, a special district sort of evolved. It's called Radio Alley. Of course, now that televisions have become so much more popular, people aren't running out trying to replace transistors every Saturday, so the shop owners had to improvise. Enter Chuck's Surplus Store. Turns out his mother is a witch and she encouraged him to open a specialty store in the back of the shop. Word got out and now he does pretty well for himself."

"A true businessman," I replied.

"You have no idea. Wait until you see his inventory." Michael gave a wink.

You can tell Radio Alley had taken a bit of a beating over the last few years. Empty storefronts and for-sale signs and phone numbers encouraging potential business owners to call for rates were posted in every other storefront. Yet a few stores remained to service the radio industry, and by far the most popular one appeared to be Chuck's. The front window was full of refurbished radios and record players in addition to a hodgepodge of items—stacked luggage, a chest of drawers, and lawn chairs. I took a closer look at the radios and even I had to smile at the name brands such as General Electric and Motorola. Much like the television style, the radios were big-boxed and either housed in wood frames with clunky knobs or with shiny candy-colored exteriors and slim dials. My favorite one was the teal one. Refurbished or not, the radios were all glossy and shiny and polished to a nth degree. Chuck took care of his appliances.

Michael hadn't been kidding about the inventory. We walked into the store and saw everything from gardening equipment—hoses, watering cans, fertilizer, trowels—to paint supplies. Chuck offered paint by the gallon, in spray cans, and even quarts of stain. Passed that was hardware with heaven knows how many nuts and bolts, and then the opposite side of the store was reserved for electronics. Chuck had crates and boxes full of wires, bulbs, dials, and knobs, all of which I assumed serviced the radios Michael had mentioned.

I looked past all the store had to offer but was still coming up short as to where the witchy supplies were. The only other thing I saw was a small entryway resembling nothing more than a broom closet. Apparently, that's where we were headed.

"Come on, let's go," Michael said, walking past the front counter and nodding a greeting to the older woman who was working as a cashier. She wore a red polyester store vest with a gold name tag pinned to it that read Marge. Her brown and silver hair was tightly curled, and her glasses had impressive thick, black frames. The woman smiled warmly.

"What can I get for you today? We have some new toasters. Top of the line, too," she said.

I had no idea what a top-of-the-line toaster looked like, but I was going to have to wait to find out.

"Actually we're going to head on back if that's all right," Michael replied, pointing to Edith's spell book, which was in my hand.

"Oh, well in that case, you'll need this." She opened the till and took out a small gold coin, about the size of a nickel, and handed it to Michael. "Chuck should be back there. Give a holler if he's not, and I'll come back and give you a hand."

"Will do. Thanks." Michael and I walked to the back of the store to the area I had just pegged as a broom closet, only I was wrong—it was a bathroom.

Michael motioned with his head that he was stepping inside, and I thought I'd, of course, wait for him in the little foyer there.

"No, c'mon," Michael said.

"In the bathroom?"

"Yes, in the bathroom. Now get in here," Michael said.

"Um, okay." I was at a loss for words. I walked in and surveyed the room. It was the type of bathroom you would expect to find in an old surplus store. The linoleum floor was cracked, the porcelain sink was chipped, and the toilet had a large rust string that I was convinced would take magic rather than cleaner to remove. Beside the bucket and mop propped up against the corner, the room was entirely empty.

Michael walked over to the toilet, flipped the coin in, and gave it a flush. He looked at me and raised his eyebrows as I waited in anticipation for whatever would happen.

The magic didn't disappoint.

As soon as the coin disappeared down the bowl, a door appeared behind us. It was as if the wall was made of gelatin and the door was pushing through from the other side. The wall opened and expanded to make room for it.

Michael turned around. "Ah, it materialized over here today. Shall we?"

"After you," I said, trying not to think about whose job it was to retrieve the gold coins from the bowels of the NYC water treatment facility.

Michael opened up the door and we stepped on through.

If I had thought the front of the store had offered a little bit of everything, it was nothing compared to what the back of the shop had in stock. One entire wall, going up about ten feet, was lined with stacked wooden planked shelves full of mason jars. The contents were floating and bobbing in various colored liquids—neon green, iridescent blue, shimmery pinks—and if I wasn't mistaking, they contained various animal parts, like bat wings and real cat eyes. I shuddered. This was old school magic all right. And it was not my cup of tea. Thankfully, the store also catered to the more modern witch and carried a selection of crystals, candles, oils, and herbs. We walked past various spell books, parchment rolls, quills, and, of course, wands on our way to pick up our supplies.

"Can I help you find anything?" The voice came from knee level. I looked down to see who had spoken and saw a black lab looking up at me.

"Ah, Chuck. Marge said you would be back here," Michael said to the lab.

The black lab wagged his tail. "I'd rather work back here like this any day than out front anymore. I can only have my ears scratched so many times, know what I'm saying?" Chuck replied.

"I hear you," Michael replied.

It was a good thing I had Agatha back at home or a talking dog would've really thrown me for a loop. You know you've been caught off guard a bit when a talking dog seems normal. Only unlike Agatha, I was betting Chuck was a shifter given what little background I knew. If that was the case, I was betting Michael had decided to stop here for more than just getting supplies.

"This is my friend Vee. She's new in town, and I was just telling her that if you don't carry it, then it doesn't exist," Michael said.

"Well, I appreciate that. We try."

"It's quite an impressive collection you have here," I said looking at the powdered dragon claws and individual vampire fangs. They reminded me of summer trips to the beach, where we would head to the seashell shop and pick up souvenirs. Instead of a jar of shark teeth sitting on the counter, Chuck had opted for vampire fangs. I left the boys to talk shop while I walked the rest of the way around and picked up the supplies that we needed, referencing Edith's spell book. Nothing was worse than getting ready to work a spell and finding out that you had forgotten one key ingredient. As I rounded up our purchases, I listened to Michael and Chuck's conversation. I had a feeling the shifter would be more willing to talk if I was out of eyesight.

"How are things in these parts?" Michael asked.

Chuck caught his meaning. "Not going to lie. A lot of us are on edge here. Even as lower-class citizens. If someone's attacking the alphas, what's gonna stop them from attacking and annihilating us?"

"Any word on who is behind it?"

"Oh sure, there's plenty of talk being thrown around. I've heard everything from rogue shifters to power-hungry witches—even a homicidal vampire got thrown into the mix. But no one has seen anything. It's all just a rumor at this point."

"What about down by the docks? Any of the rumors mention anything about the water?" Michael asked. I knew he was following up on Edith's comment that the missing girls might be near water. The only problem was Manhattan was an island.

"Can't say that they have. Why, what do you know?" Chuck looked up with his little puppy dog eyes. I rejoined the men with the supplies in hand.

"Same as you. Only rumors," Michael replied. "Give me a call though, if you hear something?"

"Was already planning on it."

"Appreciate it, Chuck." Michael then turned his attention to me. "Did you find everything?"

"That and more. Your store really is a gem," I said to Chuck.

"Thank you. You come back anytime, you hear? If you're looking for someone special, you can always let my mom know too. That's her out front, working the till."

"Will do. Thanks again."

Walking out from the back of the store was far less magical than the entrance had been. On this side of the wall, the door was already in place. Michael went to turn the lock, but the door wouldn't budge.

"What gives?" I asked, looking to see if there was a slot to put a coin in or some other trick I was missing.

"It's occupied," Michael said.

"Occupied? What do you mean?" Then I remembered what was on the other side of the door. "Oh, never mind. I got it." Someone was using the restroom. Turned out not everything in Chuck's was so magical after all.

We waited a few extra minutes before crossing through the door again. This time it opened without a hitch, and the doorway dissolved into the wall behind us as soon as we went through it. I was starting to think I needed to put some of these magical charms on my own house or maybe a ward like Michael had put on his car. I wondered how effective that would be at keeping the likes of Andrew away?

"To Penny's?" I said as I got into Michael's car with my brown Chuck's Surplus shopping bag.

"To Penny's," Michael said starting the engine.

At least this time, I didn't attempt to put on my seatbelt.

CHAPTER 13

*I*t turned out Penny's residence wasn't too far from where Mary lived and just a stone's throw from Radio Alley in Manhattan's Lower East Side. Michael parked down the block across the street from the white brick, six-story apartment building, and we surveyed the area. The buildings were all built with various colored bricks—white, red, tan, and black. The heights varied, but the metal fire escapes remained the same. This area wasn't like the nice tree-lined streets of the Upper West Side, with their fancy porches and fabric awnings.

A handful of people were out milling around, some carrying shopping bags, others looking exhausted from a long day of work, and yet others were sipping drinks on their stoops.

"Let's see if she's home, shall we?" I asked, turning to get out of the car.

Michael met me on the sidewalk, and we walked together to Penny's.

When we walked through the door, it was as if we had just walked into the food court at the mall. Without air conditioning, the apartment building was warm, and the air was thick with an odd mixture of herbs and spices, like basil, turmeric, and sage. The result was an aroma that smelled something like an Asian lasagna. It was an international food festival right here in the lower commons.

A quick look around the ground floor revealed that the apartments were set up with six units on each floor—three on each side, with the stairway zigzagging up the middle.

"What unit's hers again?" I asked Michael.

"1C. It should be the last unit on the left there." Michael pointed to the end of the hall.

We stood outside Penny's door and listened for a moment to see if we could pick up any conversation before we knocked. All seemed silent on the other end, and I let Michael go ahead and knock while we waited to see if Penny would answer.

A minute ticked by and then another.

He knocked again, and we waited some more. A young group of boys, one with a soccer ball in his arms, ran down the stairwell and beelined it for the back door. Still we stood and waited, but no sign of life was coming from the other side of the door.

Michael tried the door handle and it was locked.

"Anyone looking?" I asked with a smile on my face.

"No, but you know that I'm a member of law enforcement, right?"

"And?" I asked, drawing the word out.

"And breaking and entering is illegal."

"Then you might want to close your eyes," I said with mock seriousness as I placed my hand on the doorknob and felt the pins line up and the cylinder turn to release the lock. "Wow, I guess it was open all along. How convenient is that?" I said raising my eyebrows.

"I did not see any of this," Michael replied.

"Of course you didn't. Your eyes were closed, right?" I pushed open the door and we stepped inside.

"Holy cats," I said under my breath. Penny's apartment was a mess. Just from the doorway, I could see her couch was covered in clothes, as if she had dumped the contents of her wardrobe on top of it. Her small two-chaired kitchen table was covered with cups and bowls. Silverware littered the floor along with bathroom towels and throw pillows.

"Do you think someone tossed it?" I asked, my voice low.

Michael went into cop mode, removing the gun from the small of his back. "Stay here," he whispered as he crept along the wall to clear the apartment.

I frowned as I wasn't necessarily helpless, in case the detective had forgotten, but I was also smart and didn't feel like getting shot if whoever had ransacked Penny's apartment was still there hiding. I stood in the doorway, straining to hear anything unusual, but the only sounds reaching me were the muffled ones from neighboring apartments and the kids that lived in them.

Michael returned a minute or so later.

"All clear?" I asked.

"It is."

"Look like a trash job?"

"No, I think it's just Penny packing up. Check this out." I followed Michael as he made his way through the apartment to the teeny kitchen. Stacks of more plates were on the counter, along with the contents of her cupboards—cans of soup, cereal, peanut butter. Penny's bathroom held a similar scene and revealed her love of makeup. Her stash covered the bathroom counter and there was enough product there to restock her former employer's inventory. The waste-basket was full of discarded tubes of lipstick, broken compacts, and used false lashes. A box sat on the closed toilet seat and it too was full of beauty products. The words "bathroom" had been written across the side in black marker.

"She's moving," I said as I peeked in the bedroom and saw more half-filled boxes. "The question is why?" Why did Penny quit her job, a job she loved, and why was she packing up her apartment? Did it have something to do with the guy I saw her with last night? More questions that we needed to answer.

"Come on. Let's wait for her outside." Michael lead the way to the front door, used a handkerchief from his back pocket to wipe the doorknob free of my prints, and locked it after us.

We sat silently in the car, waiting for Penny to come home, and watched the day slip away—something I couldn't afford to do. I was eager to find answers and seeing as Penny's place wasn't giving us any, I was about to suggest we skip the stakeout and head to Michael's to work his grandmother's spell when I spotted Penny.

"There she is," I said, nodding toward the other side of the street. Penny was walking with the same guy I had seen her with the night before. She appeared to be on a little afternoon date. She was wearing an adorable white halter dress with little red cherries on it. The guy wasn't dressed quite as nice with his folded jean cuffs, black shoes, red T-shirt and Yankees baseball cap. I turned and looked at Michael as if we were having a conversation, which gave him a reason to turn toward me and watch the couple moved down the sidewalk.

"That's my guy, too. Rick Canali."

"The one you said was Melody's boyfriend?" I asked.

"I'm sure of it. He's the last person she was seen with."

"He was with Penny last night," I said. The two of them continued down the sidewalk, walking further away from us. The air shimmered around Penny and her date. Like a haze. If you could pause time and examine it closely, you'd see that it was really molecules—atoms—buzzing about them and ready to rearrange at a moment's notice. The effect was more noticeable now than ever before. I assumed it had something to do with being so close to the full moon.

"What do you want to do?" It was broad daylight. Sneaking up behind them and blasting them on their back-sides wasn't really feasible. If we did that, Michael and I would be running around town all afternoon erasing the memories of every witness, and who knows if we'd be able to catch everyone.

"Hopefully they'll head inside. Then we can make our move once they're off the street."

"Okay, smart plan," I said.

"I'm know for them every now and then."

"I'm sure you are," I replied.

Michael held my gaze. The look was smoldering, and for a second, I forgot all about Penny as I thought about what it would be like to kiss the detective. Perhaps it was the spark we had shared when we first met, or the way he looked at me, like now. Those eyes, imploring me to make a move. Or even the love he showed for his family—all of it chipped away at my hardened heart, asking me to explore the possibilities.

Perhaps just one kiss, I thought. What's the harm in that?

Michael leaned in, and instead of meeting him halfway, I came to my senses turned away. My brain won. *Oh no, Vee,* it said, *there will be no lip locking during this investigation.* I was a professional and I would contain my hormones.

"Think of Andrew," I mumbled aloud before I could help myself.

"Who is Andrew?" Michael asked, a tiny smirk on his face.

"I said that out loud?"

"You sure did. Am I stepping on someone's toes, looking at you the way I just did?"

Michael's directness caught me off guard. I hadn't imagined the look nor the intentions behind it. As if that was even a possibility. It was a good thing that neither one of us was gifted with telepathy since I was pretty sure neither one of us was thinking very pure thoughts at that moment. It was difficult to maintain your professional decorum when lust was at the helm.

"Listen—" I wasn't exactly sure what I was going to say. I couldn't tell him the truth, that whether or not I thought there was a possibility for something to develop between the two of us, it would never happen. Not because I didn't want it to, because when he looked at me like that—oh, man—I definitely did want it to, but not in the form of a one-night stand, which is what we would be left with when I zapped back to the future.

Oh, the irony of it all. I finally find a man that gets me and that I'm finding myself seriously interested in, and fate has to step in and say *nope, not going to happen*. Isn't that just a kicker? In fact, before I met Michael, I was pretty sure that the universe hadn't created my equal. That I just wasn't meant to find love in this lifetime. I had accepted it. I didn't do relationships and now here I was wishing I could.

My internal monologue came to a halt when Michael said, "I have no idea what's going on inside that head of yours, but right now, we have to move." He motioned with his head to the end of the street where Penny and Rick had stopped in the entryway of her apartment building. The single overhead bulb flicked off and on as twilight settled in. The porch step crumbled at their feet. Her date went in for a kiss and that's when we made our move.

They were already inside Penny's apartment, and we knocked on the door.

"Go away," Rick practically growled from the other side.

I could hear Penny's voice in the background. "Rick, that's not very nice."

"What, you expecting company?"

I decided to speak up in case Rick's objection prevented Penny from opening the door.

"Penny, it's me. Irene's family friend? Can I talk to you for minute?"

"Irene? I need to get this," Penny said. She opened the door for us a few seconds later. However, as soon as Rick caught sight of Michael with me, he freaked out, turning and dashing toward the window, practically hurtling himself out and down the fire escape. My arms shot out and I was ready to blast him one, but he was already out of sight. Still my fingertips emitted sparks in anticipation. Michael ran past Penny and gave chase, taking the same route but more measured.

"Rick!" Penny yelled in shock, running toward the window and looking down. Then she turned to me. "What in the stars is going on?" Penny looked nothing but confused.

"Mind if I come in? Hopefully together we can figure this out."

～

"SHE WASN'T WITH ARCHIE?"

Penny and I were standing in her kitchen, both of us keeping an eye out the window to see if we could spot Rick or Michael. So far neither one of them had returned, not that I had expected Rick to.

"No, I talked to Archie two days ago."

"Well, I have no idea where she is. I haven't seen her since ... I don't even know anymore."

"What about Rick. How long have you known him?"

Here Penny seemed less sure of herself. "A couple of

weeks. Why? What does he have to do with any of this, and why did he jump out of my window?"

I backed up.

"What do you know about the supernatural community? Archie said you were an expert."

At that compliment, Penny beamed.

"Practically everything. Witches, ghosts, shifters. What do you want to know?"

"You know Rick is a shifter then?"

"Of course I know. I thought ... well, I thought dating a werewolf might raise me up a level with my family."

"What sort of family do you have?" I asked before I could help myself. They had to be something supernatural to respect the power of a shifter.

"My parents are like you are, powerful witches, but," Penny shrugged her shoulders. "The spark just skipped right on over me. I hate being a squib," she mumbled down to the floor.

"A what?" I asked, not hearing her clearly.

"A squib, okay?" Penny blurted out. Her face flushed to match the color of her hair.

"Oh." Squibs had magical parents but no magic of their own. The result? They knew everything about the supernatural community, but their roles were always passive.

"I just wanted people to respect me. To stop feeling sorry for me."

"Feel sorry for you?"

"Poor Penny. She can't even manage a good luck charm. Look at Penny, she's such a poser."

"That's awful." I never considered how hard it must be to live around magic but not have any of your own.

"When I found out Rick was a werewolf and he was interested in me, I thought maybe he was my ticket to respect."

"Yes, about Rick."

"He's wanted by the police, isn't he? That's why he ran from the man who was with you," Penny said.

"Yes and no. You know Irene's a powerful witch, right?"

Penny nodded.

"Well, she's not the only one who's missing."

"What do you mean?"

"So far three girls are missing. Two are definitely powerful witches. I expect the third is as well."

"And?"

"We suspect the shifters might be behind it."

"Are you serious?" Penny started pacing the room. Given that the kitchen area was small, it only took two steps before she had to turn around.

"Have you heard about apex shifters being killed?" I asked gently.

Penny stopped walking and nodded.

"Well, there's a chance they might be using the witches. I don't know how exactly, but it's one idea."

"And you think Rick knows about this?"

"There's a strong possibility. He might have even been looking for another witch to grab."

"Are you kidding me? You think he was just hanging around me to see if I had magic?"

"He might have been," I said in a voice that could go either way.

Penny thrusted her fists down at her side. "Why me? Why can't anyone ever just like me for being me? It's always about magic, isn't it? Whatever happened to liking a person for their personality? Because I have a sparkling personality! Just ask any of my customers at Macy's. I'm a gem!"

"Speaking of work, why did you quit?"

"That old bat, Mrs. Finley, tried to send me to the basement again. She said my flirtatious behavior was unbecoming, so I quit. Besides, I'm out of here anyway. Rick had me reconsidering, but now more than ever I'm gone."

"Where are you going?"

"California. Warm ocean breezes and sunshine, here I come. Better yet, no one knows who I am there. I should've left years ago."

That wasn't a bad plan and it took a lot of courage to move cross country. I told Penny just as much before adding, "But before you leave, can you think of anywhere the shifters might be keeping the girls?"

Penny got silent. "I don't know. Rick never took me anywhere but the club."

"Did he ever mention any other buildings?"

"No, but I know some of his other friends. I can see what I can find out."

I didn't want Penny doing anything risky, which I had feeling she might do. Especially now knowing her desire to prove herself. "I don't think that's such a good idea," I said.

"Don't worry. Those boys are ridiculously simple." Penny batted her fake eyelashes. "I'll be smart. I promise."

I told Penny I still didn't like the idea, but she had her mind made up.

"Just be safe, okay? And here," I took my tiger's eye out of my purse and pressed it into Penny's palm. "For added protection," I said.

Penny pocketed the stone.

"Call me at the Hendrickses' or call the New York City Police Department if you learn anything. Ask for Detective Cooper," I said on my way out.

"I will, I promise," Penny said after me.

I met Michael back out front at his car. He was out of breath, hunched over, sucking in air. "Man, that kid was fast."

"I'm impressed you even attempted to run down a werewolf."

"I couldn't just let him get away without a chase." Michael stood up and I noticed his hand was bleeding.

"Your hand," I said pointing to the cut which was really bleeding at this time.

"I didn't even notice it," he said, looking at it more closely.

"It's going to need stitches," I said.

"Nah, it'll be fine."

"I don't think so..."

"Just trust me. So what did Penny have to say?"

I was still concerned with Michael's hand, but answered his question. "She didn't know anything about shifters kidnapping any witches. I found out she's a squib and she thought dating a werewolf would impress her parents."

"Wow, a squib. You don't see many of those."

"I know. Turns out it's pretty depressing growing up in the limelight. Hence, her packing up and heading west, but first, she's going to check in with Rick's friends and see if she can uncover anything."

"You think that's a good idea?"

"Not really. I gave her my tiger's eye and told her to be careful. She promised me that she would and that she'd call us if she learned anything."

Michael nodded and moved to get into his car. I followed suit and got in.

"Can you grab me a napkin from the glove box there?" Michael asked.

Again, I was thinking he needed something more than a napkin for that cut—things like antiseptic and tetanus shot came to mind, but I found a napkin and handed it over.

Michael pressed the flimsy paper to the cut and closed his eyes. I watched as he mumbled a few words and the napkin seemed to glow for a minute, and then it was all over with as quickly as it happened. Michael lifted the napkin and while he still had a cut, it was now closed and the skin pink and puffy around the edges.

"You're a healer?" I asked.

"Not really. I know a few spells," he replied.

I waited for him to elaborate.

"It helps Karen sleep better at night knowing I can fix myself up if need be."

"Your sister is smart," I replied.

"I'll tell her you think so."

CHAPTER 14

*J*t took us about twenty minutes with traffic to reach Michael's apartment. The location wasn't quite Lower Manhattan, but it wasn't Midtown either.

"The apartment isn't much, but I'm close to my precinct," Michael said, unlocking the plain black wooden door.

"Which one is that?" I asked, walking in after him.

"Sixth. It's just up 10th Street here." Michael tossed his keys on the counter and kicked off his shoes like I imagined he did every time he came home. I followed suit, taking off my own shoes.

The detective's apartment was the size of a shoebox, and I am only slightly exaggerating. It was one room—kitchen, living room, bedroom—all in one. The bathroom was down the hall. Michael lifted up his hide-a-bed and pushed it into the wall, securing it with the latch. Now the room had slightly more floor space, but there was no place to sit.

"Sorry, I usually only sleep here," Michael said, and I knew he was telling the truth. The apartment was sparse, lacking the personal touches that a home usually had. I had a feeling if Mary was let loose in here she would have it feeling warm and cozy in no time. As it was now, the only personal item that stood out was a small black-and-white TV and a chest of drawers. A refrigerator and a single hotplate with a drip coffee maker was the extent of the detective's appliances.

Michael unbuttoned his shirt sleeves and rolled them up.

I set up the candles as Edith's spell required. A black one was in the center, a gray one in front and behind it. A yellow one to the left and a purple one to the right.

"You ready to do this?" Michael asked.

"Let's crack that shield," I replied.

Michael lit the incense and then the black candle. Heads together, we read Edith's spell:

> *Here stands the enemy all alone*
> *They are without friend*
> *Without help*
> *I pity thee.*

Then I lit the gray candles and together we said:

> *Here lies sickness, doubt and worry*
> *It draws closer to you.*
> *Then the green and purple candles:*
> *Your new-found friend is fear*
> *and tension marches by your side.*
> *Do you hear them?*
> *They are coming.*

WE SAT THERE for a few minutes, per Edith's instructions, allowing the candles to burn and the spell to reach its target.

"You ready to see if it worked?" he asked me.

I nodded.

Then Michael took my hands. The shock was expected. Warmth spread from my fingertips down to my toes. Like an electrical current with no outlet, the static built, buzzing through my veins. The feeling was electrifying to say the least, but I didn't let go.

White light surrounded the world around us. Then the visions came. It was as if we were watching a movie being fast-forwarded. I took slow, calming breaths in hopes that my steady breathing would slow the vision down. But as my breath slowed, the channel changed. The movie did slow, but it wasn't showing me pictures of Irene or Melody. No, I was seeing Michael as a young boy, shooting sparks out of his fingers, and then laughing as he attempted to alter his own memory, but instead ended up shooting himself backwards on his behind. I looked up at Michael and saw that he was lost in his own movie and I wondered if his was playing a matinee of my life. That would be trickier as he was bound to notice the world looked a bit different.

I squeezed his hand. "We need to focus together," I said. The individual movies streamed together, and the channel changed once more.

We were in the capturer's mind.

The insatiable desire for power came through, but so did the fear. Our spell was already causing the capturer to doubt themselves.

"Is three witches enough?" the person asked. "What if the spell isn't right? Can I trust the calculations? If I'm wrong, my life will be ruined. My career will be over!"

I tried to push outside of the capturer's mind to see if we could get a visual on the person or their surroundings, but we were trapped inside the capturer's mind. The fears continued to build until they panicked. "I can't do this. I need more power!" Then the person screamed. It was a feral cry. The shock forced Michael and I to let go.

We sat there, stunned by what had just happened. Fear crept inside my head too.

"What if our spell backfired?" I said quietly to Michael.

"What do you mean?" he asked, his brow furrowed.

"What if they hurt the girls or kidnap another one for more power?"

Michael stared off into the distance.

The phone rang a couple of feet away in the kitchen. At first, I blocked it out, but it continued to ring, cycle after cycle, until neither one of us could ignore it anymore.

"Cooper here," Michael said when he answered it. "I see. Where at? No, don't send Mulroney. No, I will be there. Just give me ten minutes to make the drive." Michael hung up the phone and looked at me. "Blow out those candles and let's go. I have a new case. Homicide."

TRUE TO HIS WORD, ten minutes later we were pulling up to the crime scene.

"Oh no," I said as Michael's car came to a stop at the curb. Unless Rick had a doppelgänger, that was his body lying face-down, dead on the pavement.

"What?" Michael asked, craning his neck over the steering wheel.

"Look at your vic. It's Rick, isn't it?" I said. Even I was surprised that I had been able to identify the victim from the car.

"Cripes, you're right." Michael rubbed his eyes.

"That makes another shifter down," I said.

"And he's werewolf."

We got out of the car together, Michael walking right into the center where the uniforms were waiting, standing guard over the body, while I took to the fringes of the action. The scene had already started to draw a crowd. I stood there silently and listened to see what other information I could glean from the bystanders talking around me.

"Heard he was attacked from behind," one young kid said.

"What, like a robbery? Everyone knows Rick don't have no money," the other teenager replied.

I turned to the group of boys and interrupted them. "You know the guy?" I said motioning to the dead body.

"Rick? Of course we know Rick. The question is, who are you?" the first boy asked.

"Oh, I'm just visiting from out of town and wondering what I need to look out for around here," I said, clutching my handbag closer to me as if I was worried about being mugged right then and there.

"Nah, you have nothing to worry about here. Rick could've got snubbed for a hundred different reasons."

"Anyone see it go down?" I asked.

"You sure you're not a cop?" the second kid asked.

"Do I look like a cop?" I asked them.

They both nodded their heads. "Uh-huh," they said in unison.

That got a smile out of me. "Well, I promise you that I'm not."

The teenagers looked at one another, mumbling something back and forth before coming to some mutual conclusion.

"All I heard is that it happened real quick. One minute Rick is walking down the street and the next, bang, he's dead," the first kid said.

"He was shot?" I asked.

"Did I say he was shot?" the first kid asked

"You said bang," his friend said.

"Nah, he wasn't shot. I just meant that it happen in an instant."

I nodded. "Got it. So it happened really fast."

"Right, that's what I said," the first kid replied.

Michael left the scene and walked toward us. "Vee, come here?" he said to me.

"I thought you said you ain't a cop," the second kid called after me.

"I'm not, I swear," I said over my shoulder as I accompanied Michael across the street. Neither one of the boys seemed to believe me if the scowl on their faces was any indication.

"What did you learn?" Michael asked me.

"Kid said it happened real quick, though no one can make an ID on the perp."

"What do you make of this?" Michael nodded to the body, which was still lying face down. There were no visible marks, but a tourniquet was tied tightly around his upper arm and a syringe cap was next to it. Somebody took his blood. The question was, why?

Michael and I looked at one another. "What do you know about shifter blood?" I asked quietly.

"Only what it sells for on the black market. They call it Werewild. Junkies love it for the high."

I had heard that as well. "You think there's some sort of homicidal drug dealer out there?" I asked. I supposed it was a possibility. People killed each other for drugs all the time, but that didn't explain our missing witches.

"Could be. I'm going to check with the other precincts. See if they've seen an uptick in Werewild arrests."

I nodded.

"Listen, I'm going to be here a long time. Why don't you take my car, and I'll catch up with tomorrow?" Michael offered. I eyed his car. It really was a thing of beauty. Well, when it didn't have the ugly ward on it.

"No, that's okay. I can take the subway back. Thanks though."

"No, I insist."

"Really, I'm fine." I could tell Michael was trying to be chivalrous, but it really wasn't necessary. Then again, I didn't have a ton of cash left. Michael must have sensed my hesitation. He threw his car keys to me without another word.

CHAPTER 15

I got back to the Hendrickses' apartment and let myself in. It was late, and the rooms were dark. I hadn't bothered to leave a light on, but I wished that I would have. As a reflex, my power surged to the surface. I was ready to take down any threat that made itself known.

I walked through the kitchen and into the living room, stopping to turn on the lamp. In a second, the room was flooded in soft light and a man's voice came from behind me.

"I thought you'd never come home," he said. I whipped around and about blasted George through all of his nine lives. As it was, I hadn't been able to hold all my power back, and the carpet was now singed about a foot in front of him.

"What the what?" I said down to the cat. "You can talk?"

George stretched out into the carpet. "Now don't go telling me a witch like yourself has never heard of a familiar." His voice was like his personality—slow moving.

"No, I'm well acquainted with your type, having one of my own back home. I just had no idea that you were one yourself."

George stretched again and started raking his claws on

the carpet in a rhythmic pattern. Apparently, he had decided not to comment.

I pressed on. "Do you know what happened to Irene?"

"Well, I did hear some commotion the other day. It woke me up from my midmorning nap." George left it at that.

"And?" I said drawing the word out and hopefully his explanation.

"And what? The noise woke me from my nap and then I went back to sleep." I had a feeling George had been a cat for far too long and his human tendencies were now long forgotten. Still, I tried to spark his memory. "Do you know if it was another woman's voice you heard or maybe it was a man?"

"I think it was just Mr. Hendricks. He was fighting with Irene, but there's nothing new there."

"Mr. Hendricks," I said again. I walked down the hall to the man's study.

"Hey, what about my dinner?" George shouted after me, with a couple of meows thrown in for good measure. I ignored his pleas. It wasn't like he would starve in ten minutes and it served him right for not telling me earlier that he was a familiar.

Mr. Hendricks' doorknob unlocked at my touch, and I went inside.

"What secrets are you keeping?" I said aloud. Again, I used the summoning spell that I had used earlier when searching the office, only this time I asked it to reveal Mr. Hendricks' secrets.

At the end of the incantation, the tapestry of the periodic table of elements waved from a magical breeze and then rolled up like a shade, revealing a chalkboard covered in research. Geometric diagrams, pictures, and equations filled every inch of the chalkboard. Words like elixir of life, immortality, essence of life, with blood written in parentheses, along with different minerals and their organic compositions, filled the board. Underlined in big bold letters was, NEED MORE POWER.

The clues could only mean one thing: Mr. Hendricks was an alchemist. In addition to being obsessed with gold, alchemists sought to create the philosopher's stone, which was said to not only turn base metals into gold but also allow for everlasting life.

Then I thought back to earlier tonight when we were inside the capturer's mind. The person had been worried about their life's work being for naught. Mr. Hendricks' impressive calculations on the chalkboard certainly fit that description.

A flood of questions poured into my mind. If Mr. Hendricks had kidnapped the young witches, had he really taken Mrs. Hendricks to the Catskills or was it possible that she was in on it too? I didn't think so, but I also saw firsthand how impressive she was at lying. In the corner of the chalkboard were three words that pretty much solidified Mr. Hendricks' guilt. It read, power equals Irene. It seemed that his research had identified that he needed a power source, and a supernatural one at that.

Then I thought back to the dead shifters and made the blood connection. Mr. Hendricks was somehow going to use the shifters' blood and the witches' power to make the philosopher's stone. It was the biggest lightbulb moment of the case and yet I still had no idea where the young witches were being kept. I raced out of Mr. Hendricks' office and hunted down George. He was looking wistfully at his food bowl.

"Are you gonna feed me yet or what?" the cat asked.

"One more thing," I said.

If cats could roll their eyes, I had a feeling George would.

"Again with the questions. Please, I'm starving here." He threw in a couple pitiful meows as evidence.

"The Catskills, what do you know about them?" I asked.

"Do they have cats there?"

"I'm serious. I need to find out if the Hendrickses are really there."

"I wouldn't know nothing about that. Mary always prepared the house."

"Mary ..." I raced to the phone and quickly retrieved the telephone book, flipping through the pages until I found Mary's home phone number. It was late, but I couldn't do anything about that. This was far too important to worry about being polite.

Mary's line rang and rang, but there was no answer. I wondered where on Earth she could be at ten o'clock at night with an ailing mother at home. She could have turned off the phone ringer so it wouldn't disturb her mother, much like Mr. Hendricks had asked me to do this morning. Come to think of it, the phone ringer here was still turned off. I turned the phone upside down and switched it back on. With Mary not answering her phone, there was only one thing left to do—pay Mary a late-night visit.

I threw a handful of kibble into George's bowl and started to leave the apartment once more.

"What, no cold cuts?" George hollered after me.

I ignored him and locked the door after me. Henry greeted me once more in the elevator.

"You know what, I just thought of something," he said. "I did see Irene on Monday morning. She was going out to breakfast with Mr. Hendricks. I remember I was surprised they were going anywhere because the young miss didn't look too well."

I was right. Mr. Hendricks had taken Irene hostage. As if I needed more evidence.

"What do you mean, she didn't look well?" I asked.

"She looked tired. I remembered Mr. Hendricks kept his arm around her waist."

That was good to know. "Thanks much," I said and stepped out of the elevator and into the night.

～

MARY OPENED THE DOOR, clearly alarmed. Her cornflower blue eyes were bright and wide like their namesake.

She was wearing a nightgown with a sheer robe over it. Her long blonde hair was down and wavy, ending just past her shoulders. Worry lines creased between her eyebrows.

"What's wrong?" Mary asked upon seeing that I was the one knocking so late at night.

I hesitated. I wasn't sure how much I wanted to involve Mary, for her sake. But something had to account for me showing up at her apartment close to midnight and asking about the Hendrickses' summer residence.

"I have to find the Hendrickses. It's about Irene, and they went to the Catskills this morning. Do you have any idea where they're staying? Do they stay at a certain resort every summer or ..."

"Oh no, nothing like that. Mr. Hendricks doesn't believe in socialized activities. You'll never see him at a themed dinner."

That I could see. "So where is it exactly?" I asked.

"In the mountains. A little less than two hours away," Mary answered.

I was going to need more directions than that. "Is it by a certain landmark or do you have an address?"

"It's by the North Ridge Resort. That way Mr. Hendricks can drop Madeline off and she can get her fill of society while he enjoys the peace and tranquility of the lake and mountains."

I had never been a guest at the type of resort Mary was describing, but I had seen the movie *Dirty Dancing*, so I had a general gist of what she was referencing. Hokey entertainment, like magic shows and hula-hoop contests, and games like Simon Says and countless trips to the beauty salon to try on wigs dominated the daily schedule.

"North Ridge Resort," I repeated out loud. "Is it hard to find?"

"You can't possibly be thinking about heading there right now?" Mary's voice was incredulous.

"Actually, I am. It's imperative that I speak with them." More like, it was imperative that I tracked down Mr. Hendricks and see where he was keeping his daughter and the other witches captive. Heaven forbid, I was too late. I had no idea how he had planned to transfer the witches' power into a stone. I had a feeling that it wouldn't be gentle.

The worry in Mary's forehead creased even deeper. I couldn't help it if she didn't like my plan. She had no idea who I really was or what I was there to do.

CHAPTER 16

*T*en minutes later and with a rough set of directions on how to get to the Hendrickses' summer home, I set back off in Michael's car. Speaking of Michael, I decided to swing by his apartment and see if he was home yet. Best case, he could ride shotgun. Worst case, I would leave a note on his door. I'd hate to just disappear with his car into the dead of night, never to be heard from again. After all, I was planning on jumping back to the future after I solved this case, which if all went well, would be in a few short hours.

It turned out Michael wasn't home yet. I scribbled a quick note with a pencil and scrap piece of paper that I had found in his glove box. It read: Took your car to the Catskills. Tracking down the Hendrickses. Think Mr. is our bad guy.

I signed my name and slipped the note under the door and backtracked to Michael's car, ready to hit the road. But first, a quick stop at the gas station. My funds were teetering dangerously low, and I had just enough cash to fill the car's gas tank and grab some late-night snacks for the road trip.

THE TWO-LANE ROAD curved steeply up the mountain. Pine trees were on one side and a steep drop-off was on the other. I had visions of chasing Mr. Hendricks back down this treacherous road and fighting to maintain control of the car as he swerved and attempted to out run me. Thankfully, in Michael's car, that was highly unlikely. Along the highway, some of the houses had signs with things like "Shelters Cove/Established 1934," or simple signs such as "The Millers" with a cartoon bear or a rainbow trout painted on them. They were meant to let guests know which cabin they had rented or for homeowners to show off their properties. The Hendrickses', however, was marked only with a regular address sign and a practical reflector. I didn't want to roll up in their driveway and announce that they had company. So I passed by their entrance and drove down to a neighboring cabin, choosing to pull into their driveway instead and walk through the woods toward the house.

Seeing as it was summertime in the Catskills, almost all of the cabins were occupied and the house that I was approaching was no different. Only this house was in full party mode, and I highly doubted there was an adult in sight. Not that it hadn't been sanctioned. It wasn't unheard of for the parents of rich kids to open their homes to these wild summer soirées. The driveway was packed with cars, and the front yard was littered with people and empty beer cans. Music rolled out the front open windows as did laughter. It was a perfect cover, as I highly doubted anyone would pay any attention to me. The only thing these kids would care about was if someone called the police and busted up their party, which was just the sort of thing Mr. Hendricks would do if he knew what was happening next door to him.

I parked Michael's car, and the moment I got out with my purse and stood in the gravel driveway, my senses went on higher alert. I assumed it had to do with the fact that I was in close proximity to the missing witches, but as soon as I started to make my way through the wooded lot that separated the homes, my senses pulled me back toward the party house. At first, I wasn't sure if I was reading my feelings right. I'd take two or three steps toward the Hendrickses' property and then stop and take inventory of how I felt. Time after time, my body and intuition told me to go back toward the party house. It didn't make sense, but I learned a long time ago to trust my intuition. So, I listened to it and backtracked toward the house, retracing my steps until I was back at Michael's car.

"Okay, what is it that you want me to see?" I asked myself. I opened my intuition up and stood there in the driveway. Hidden in shadow, I surveyed the scene and waited for something to jump out at me. A group of guys, teenagers really, were standing in the middle of the yard just off the porch. With their varsity jackets on and slicked-back hair, they were the epitome of the high school cool kids club. Nothing about their behavior, except that it was a bit obnoxious, jumped out at me. So I moved on, scanning the group of girls sitting on the porch swing, sipping drinks out of plastic cups and giggling like fools. They, of course, were watching the group of guys not thirty feet away. The girls' admiring looks made me feel slightly sorry for them. Don't waste your time on a boy like that, I wanted to warn them. Not that they would listen, but hey, it would make my conscious feel better if I gave them a warning. Of course, nothing nefarious was going on there either. I stood there, biting my bottom lip and wondering what in the world my intuition wanted me to see. Certainly, I wasn't opposed to teenaged summer parties. I knew that underage drinking was frowned upon, but I highly doubted my witchy sense was encouraging me to call the cops to report such behavior. No, there had to be something else that I just wasn't seeing yet.

Then upstairs in the second story of the house, I saw it. A green flash. It lasted just long enough to have me look up in the window. I stood there for a minute, waiting to see if it would happen again. After a few seconds passed, I started to question if I had really seen anything at all and then there it was again—the green flash. Something supernatural was definitely going on upstairs. Now it was up to me to find out what it was. The only problem was I was practically old enough to be the parent of one of these kids. At least I was short. Generally, I didn't see my height as an advantage, but in this case, I was more than happy to be vertically compact.

The last thing I wanted was for the partygoers to think that their party was being busted. That would create chaos as the teenagers tried to flee and I was far less likely to walk in on whatever was happening upstairs. My powers hummed and cracked on my fingertips as I kept my head low and made my way to the house. Luckily, everyone was so absorbed in their own conversations and under the influence of alcohol to pay much attention to me. I grabbed a discarded cup that had been left on the entry table and used it as a prop as I weaved my way through the crowd and found the staircase that headed up. There were groups of teenagers here as well, even one couple engaged in a lip-lock session about four steps up. I politely sidestepped them and over others as I went upstairs. My powers peaked, as did my curiosity, the closer I came to the landing.

"Oh my goodness, that is wicked cool. Show us again," a girl's voice practically shrieked. I had my shoulder against the wall and my feet crossed as I stood outside a bedroom and listened in.

"Are you for real? Dude, this is way freaky," said another girl.

"I think you need an exorcism," another girl added in all seriousness.

"Shut up, no she doesn't." the first girl replied. "Don't you get it? She's a witch. Magic is real."

"I don't know. I don't like it. I'm out of here," I looked inside the room just in time to see a girl perform an impressive hair flip and head toward me. I turned and looked behind me and held the drink to my mouth as the girl made her exit. She completely blew past me and headed down the stairs.

"Don't listen to Betty. She's just jealous because the only thing she can conjure is a credit card," said the one girl.

"And it's her daddy's," the second girl added.

That got a laugh out of the trio.

"Thanks. I know it's sort of freaky, but it's kind of cool, right?" the young witch asked her friends.

"It's totally cool."

"Totally," the two girls chimed in one after the other.

"What's your aunt think?" the first girl asked.

"Aunt Carol? Are you kidding me? She has no clue what's happening to me. She's too busy trying to seduce the dance instructor back at the resort," the young witch replied. Oh my goodness, so it was true. *Dirty Dancing* was based on a true story, I thought to myself.

"But don't, like, witches run in families or is that just a myth?" the second girl asked.

"I have no idea. It's not like they have a witchcraft section at the public library or that I can ask my parents. They're dead, in case you forgot."

"No, course I didn't forget. I'm sorry. I just thought maybe you knew," the second girl said.

"The only thing I know is green sparks sometimes come out of my fingertips and I swear one time I froze Mr. Giggles in place for a minute. Don't worry, the pug was okay," the witch quickly added.

I suddenly knew why my intuition had brought me here.

This poor young witch needed direction much like the other young witches I was searching for. And if this young lady wasn't careful, she might face the same predicament that the other young witches found themselves in—at the hand of someone with much sinister intentions than showing off at a party.

"Let's go get drinks," the first girl said.

"Yeah, who knows what Betty is telling everybody downstairs right now," the second girl added.

"We better go and make it sound like she's crazy," the first girl laughed, and the trio moved to come out of the bedroom. Thankfully, the young witch was in the back of the line, and I was able to tap her on the shoulder as she walked by.

"Can I have a quick word?" I said.

"Um," the girl shook her head as if unsure of what to say.

I pressed on, pulling her aside into the room that she had just left. "I overheard your conversation."

The girl started shaking her head more vigorously, and I had a feeling she was trying to come up with an excuse for what I might have overheard.

"It's okay, I'm a fellow witch. In fact, it was your little magical show that drew me to you." I pointed to the window, and the girl's face drained of color. "I just wanted to let you know you have to be careful out there. There's a big supernatural world just waiting for you to discover it, but you want to discover it on your own terms and not when some demon and shifter comes calling, drawn by your magical talents." I may have pushed that last comment a bit too far as the girl looked like she was about to start hyperventilating. I touched her arm in a calming manner. For a split second, I did think about erasing her memory and taking back what I had just said, but then again, it was smart for her to be armed with the knowledge of what existed out there. She was going to be part of the witchcraft community, of that I was certain.

I continued. "Don't worry, it's not all things that go bump in the night. There's plenty of witches out there, good ones. In fact, more than plenty if you live anywhere near New York City."

The girl looked hopeful. "Really?"

"Really. I promise." I took out Michael's phone number from my purse and gave it to the girl. I remembered him telling me that he had introduced Melody to a coven, and I was sure he would be able to do the same for this young girl. If anyone knew the ins and outs of the supernatural community in New York City, it was him. "This guy can help you out. Just call him and tell him that Vee told you to call. He can introduce you to the right friends."

"Thanks," the girl said, pocketing the number. "But why can't you just help me?"

I could tell she was still a bit shaken by my demon and shifter comment.

"Because I have another witch to help. Speaking of which, I need to get going." I gave the girl's hand a squeeze and left her to join her friends, hoping that she would take my advice to heart.

I was one foot out the front door when I heard Betty's voice come from the adjacent room.

"Marge is a freak, and I'm going to make sure everybody else knows that."

"What is your problem, Betty? You can't handle that somebody has a special talent that you don't?" one of the young witch's friends replied.

"Talent? You call what Marge can do a talent? That's witchcraft. You know they used to burn people at the stake for doing things like that. Maybe I can bring it back." Betty looked down at her fingernails as if she was contemplating doing just that.

Oh no, I thought. There was no way I was walking out of

that house when girls like Betty were out to destroy a young girl's life. It's hard enough being a young witch and figuring out your own powers without having a bully like Betty out to destroy you.

I walked right into that room and looked Betty straight in the eye. The other two girls sucked in a breath, not even knowing who I was. Just my mere presence seemed to tell them that I meant business.

Betty wasn't that smart.

"And who are you?" she said with her snotty attitude.

Oh man, the choices. It would give me nothing but satisfaction to blast Betty and her backside. Unfortunately, it would also not cause her to change her ways. If anything, she would be more inclined to run around telling everyone about how horrible Marge was and how she needed to be stopped. No, I had to be the adult here. I took Betty by the wrist. She looked at me in shock that I had dared to touch her.

"Let me—"

I didn't let her get in another word. I sent a thousand volts from my body into hers and instantly recircuited her brain, making her forget everything that she had witnessed upstairs, including her promises to ruin Marge's life. The other two friends stood silently.

I took a play out of Michael's book and said, "You know, Betty, I don't think you really like being in the Catskills anymore. No, you want to make a difference in other people's lives. So you're going to join the Peace Corps." It was the only thing I could think of on the fly that may give Betty a glimpse at how ridiculous and petty she was being. Perhaps working toward world peace would open her eyes and make her a better person. It was either that or I was going to have her join a monastery. I decided the Peace Corps was a more practical option.

"You're going to go ahead and contact them tomorrow morning and see about enlisting. Do you understand me?" I asked.

"Peace Corps," Betty said numbly.

I nodded my head. "Good. And, you are going to be very nice to these two young ladies here," I raised my eyebrows to them.

"Penny," girl number one said.

Of course that was her name.

"Judy," said the second girl.

"You're going to be very nice to Penny and Judy, and their friend Marge. Got it?" I said to Betty.

Once again, Betty nodded.

"Good. You should probably head home now so you can start preparing to join the Peace Corps," I said letting go of Betty's arm.

She blinked her eyes a couple of times and didn't say another word as she walked out the front door. I then turned my attention to Judy and Penny. "Betty won't remember anything about Marge. The question is, can Marge trust you?"

"Absolutely," said Penny.

"Totally. Marge is our girl," Judy replied.

"Good, I'd hate to have to encourage you to join the Peace Corps as well." Both Judy and Penny turned white as snow.

"We'll be good, I promise," Penny said.

"I trust that you will be," I said with perhaps a little bit more conviction than I felt.

With my good deed done for the day, it was now time to rescue some witches. I walked out of the house with my shoulders back and my head held high, no longer caring if my presence caused pandemonium or not.

I crept through the woods separating the two properties. With my knees bent and my body crouched low, I weaved through the underbrush, careful to stay alert for any incoming threats. The night was eerily quiet and the moon full and high in the sky. In the distance, somewhere in the mountains, a werewolf howled and sent a shiver down my spine.

Then through the tree line, I saw the Hendrickses' house. Lights were on, but the question was, who was home? I stuck to the property's edge as I walked downhill and around to the back of the yard. From there, I looked up at the house, which was set slightly on a hill. In front of me, I saw it—a garden shed. I knew that's where the girls were hidden. It made perfect sense. The setting was isolated with very few neighbors, and it was in close proximity to the water, not twenty feet from the lake's edge. And who could forget the dirt? I would bet any amount of money that the shed had a dirt floor. There was only one way to find out if my hunches were correct.

My adrenaline was pulsing as I felt I was moments away from rescuing the girls. I kept my head low and dashed across the backyard until I was in front of the shed, my body hidden from the front of the house in shadow. With ease, I put my hand on the shed door and felt it unlock in my grasp. Carefully I pushed the door inward and leaned in to look inside.

And that was when someone attacked me.

I had been so focused on the shed that I hadn't heard the person sneak up behind me. Without warning, my neck was gripped from behind and searing hot pain poured into my body like lava. The unexpected pain took me to my knees. I fought through the pain and tried to reach behind me and get ahold of my attacker. One fistful was all I needed to fry their circuits. I tried to conjure an orb of electricity to hit them with, but my power was quickly fading. Then, it was lights out.

CHAPTER 17

*C*olors swirled and melted together in front of my
face—watery blues, soft lilacs, cotton candy pink.
Unable to focus, I watched the colors dance in front of me. In
the distance, or maybe it was right beside me, I heard voices,
but I couldn't concentrate on them. I had no idea what they
were saying. Every time someone spoke, the colors became
more vibrant, pulsing with the cadence of speech. I remembered thinking that I must be drugged, although I didn't
remember the how or when. I only remembered the burning
pain. Then, I shut my eyes and I slept.

The only good thing about being drugged was that it
made it easier to have an out-of-body experience, which is
what astral projection required and what I was attempting to
do to call for backup. Reaching out to my familiar, Agatha,
was my best shot at getting her to alert Lexi and the other
time-traveling witches. When you used astral projection,
your physical body remained unconscious in one spot while
you projected yourself to another. The fact that I had to pick
not only another place to project to but also another time
made it all the more of a challenge and why I'd be able to

accomplish it only through Agatha. My eyes were already closed and my head felt fuzzy. I used that to my advantage as I floated away, feeling myself lift up from my body and, like a current, let the pull of the future take me away. Colors blurred past my eyes, much like the ones that had swarmed in front of my face a minutes before, only now additional hues joined the fold. It was like I was being churned in a vat of rainbow sherbet.

Slowly, my living room came into focus, and there was Agatha, lying on my kitchen table just snoozing away.

"Agatha," I said, my voice echoing in my ears. Agatha lifted up her paw and used it to cover her ear as to not be disturbed.

"Agatha!" I said, louder this time. She continued to rub her ear, but this time she cracked open an eye. Seeing my projection had her coming fully alert. Her head jerked up and both eyes popped open.

"What's wrong? Where are you?" Agatha asked.

"In a shed in the Catskills. The Hendrickses' summer home. Get backup, quickly!"

The words were barely out of my mouth before Agatha leapt off the kitchen table and into action. My living room dissolved in front of my face and I felt myself being pulled backwards through the ether until I was sucked back into my own body.

A COLD, hard slap across my face brought me to. My cheek stung. The colors were still there, but my mind was coming back. My hands were chained behind my back. My throat was dry, my head ached, and I felt weak. I looked down at my torn dress and bare feet.

"Get up!" the woman snapped at me. I lifted my head,

blinking several times as Mary's face came into focus. "Walk," she commanded me.

I twisted my wrists in their metal vice, recalling the rope that had held the other girls secure.

"I'm not taking any more chances," Mary replied as if reading my mind. But little did Mary know, I could break out of handcuffs quicker than I could have with rope. After all, mechanical locks were no match for me.

Mary grabbed my arm to lead me forward. The same searing pain filled my body and threatened to take me down once more. She gave a wicked laugh, and if my strength was half of what it usually was, I would break out of the handcuffs and throttle her.

My legs were wobbly as I staggered forward up the hill and toward the house. Outside, shifters stood watch, their arms folded across their chests and their eyes steely. I had no idea what they shifted into, but I had a feeling it wasn't puppy dogs.

The air shimmered and flickered around them. Their hands twitched. *It was a full moon,* I thought, which only made things more dangerous for us. The shifters were forced to change before the sun came up, that was just the way they were made. Preventing them from doing so would be catastrophic for all of us close by. I shivered as I thought about the house full of teenagers next door.

Mary nudged me forward. The shifters stepped aside, and I walked into the ground level of the Hendrickses' Catskills home. The house was full of rustic charm. It was all exposed cedar—the walls, ceiling, and floor. Of course, it would be sometime before I would remember what the place had looked like. At that time my only concern was not dying. The room was a living room and kitchen combo. The living room furniture had been pushed back except for a small end table, leaving the center of the floor open where a geometrical pattern had been painted. I recognized the pattern from Mr. Hendricks' chalkboard. The three teenage witches sat bound there in the center. Like me, their hands were behind their backs, bound in handcuffs. Mary must've had to adapt her bounding strategies after Irene demonstrated her fire power —which I was sure she did shortly after being captured.

"Didn't I tell you to stay out of this?" she said as she led me to the center of the floor and sat me down among the other three girls. She then used an electrical cord to bind us all together. Only our feet were free. Then she removed a dagger from the fireplace mantel, where a fire crackled below it. The room was already warm from the summer nighttime air, the fire only added to it, making me sweat.

My mind struggled to comprehend how Mary could be the mastermind behind this. Across the room in the kitchen, Mr. and Mrs. Hendricks had been tied to kitchen chairs. The chairs were back to back, with their hands behind the chairs and tied together. Handkerchiefs had been used to gag their mouths. Tears streamed down Madeline's face.

"I am more than just a kitchen witch. I have given my life in servitude to your family and now you will give to me what I deserve." Mary knelt down in front of Mr. Hendricks. "My mother used to rule New York City and once this stone heals her, she will rule it once more with me by her side."

I couldn't believe that Mary had orchestrated all of this to regain her mother's strength. On one hand, it was an act of love, trying to save her mother, but somewhere along the line, it had gone horribly wrong and twisted into one of the most malicious plots I had ever come across.

Mary stood and held the dagger up to Mr. Hendricks' face. "I'm going to cut you free and you're going to make the stone. If you make one move toward those doors, those shifters will shred you." The man standing guard smiled as if that was something they would thoroughly enjoy.

Once the gag was free from his mouth, Mr. Hendricks tried to reason with Mary. "Listen, Mary, I don't know how to make the stone. It's all theory at this point and without my notes—"

"I don't want to hear your excuses! You will make that stone, or I will kill you all right here, right now!"

Mr. Hendricks visibly swallowed.

Mary led Mr. Hendricks to the center of the circle, to the small table where chunks of raw minerals and tools for measurement stood. He eyed them skeptically.

Mary retrieved five glass vials from the fireplace mantle. "Five vials should be enough, don't you think?" she said winking at me. I quickly surmised that she was planning to take blood from all of the witches present—herself included. Unlike the werewolves, I doubted she was going to use a syringe. Light glinted off the dagger in her hand.

She started with her own wrist. I looked away, but the smell of the blood put the already tense shifters over the edge. I looked up and saw that two of them had partially changed. Their hands were now paws and their teeth elongated. One shifter whimpered, and his back leg pawed at the ground.

This was incredibly stupid, I thought to myself, employing the shifters to act as security. Although, I had a feeling these guys had been ordered to comply and that they hadn't volunteered for the job. No werewolf would willfully offer to take such a job on a full moon. They must be low in the rank.

I caught a look between the three teenage girls. The look meant that they were ready to act. They were done being prisoners and playing this game. Unfortunately, I wasn't in on the plan, but I knew I had to be ready to fight. I took a second to undo my handcuffs. With my hands hidden behind my back, Mary was completely oblivious to what was going on right in front of her. Then, I touched each of the others girls' handcuffs, releasing them as well.

Irene gave a nod and while Mary was still adding her own blood to a vile, Melody wiggled her arms free and shot out a forceful orb shield that knocked everyone backward except the six of us, who were safe within the circle for now. Essentially, we were trapped inside a strong protective bubble. The shifters had fully changed, and they were snapping and snarling, trying to penetrate the bubble. I didn't know how long we had until they broke through.

The electrical cord did nothing to bind us together. Once Melody loosened it, it fell off with ease. I took advantage of this newfound weapon and plugged the electrical cord into a nearby outlet. Using my power to manipulate electricity, I turned the cord into an electrically charged lasso. It was time for me to wrangle a bad guy.

At that moment, Lexi and Nuala broke through the front door. The timing couldn't have been more perfect if we had planned it. True to their special abilities, Lexi had been able to locate me with the extra senses she had been blessed with, and Nuala immediately got to work kicking some werewolf butt. Out of the corner of my eye, I could see Lexi hurling objects telepathically through the air. The toaster oven, coffee pot, and frying pan all flew off the kitchen counter and beat one of the werewolves into submission. Nuala showed off her boxing skills, using the other werewolf like a punching bag. He was down for the count in thirty seconds flat.

Mr. Hendricks took cover under the small table. It wasn't large enough to protect his whole body, and his feet stuck out from under it. The three witches each took turns throwing magical ailments Mary's way. It turned out Mary had powerful fire capabilities as she hurled fireball after fireball at the lot of us. Melody's shield of protection popped, and the chaos from outside the bubble flooded in.

I circled my lasso above my head and directed it toward Mary. The look on her face when the cord made its mark was priceless. A look of shock registered, followed by anger as she still managed to flip her palms forward and throw off fireball after fireball.

At that instant, Michael walked through the door. He was in full cop mode, gun drawn, and ready to take someone down.

Knowing she would be going down, Mary took one last shot, aimed at Michael. His attention was drawn to the werewolves Nuala and Lexi were still engaging in hand-to-hand combat. The moment one went down, another one came too. What did I say? Shifters were tough to keep down for long.

I simultaneously threw a lightning bolt while diving in front of Michael, getting hit with the fireball that had been intended for him. The orb blasted through me, and it felt like being stabbed with a hot poker. Fortunately, my lightning bolt was a bull's-eye and Mary crumpled to the ground. Not so fortunately, so did I.

Michael rushed to my side while my fellow witches subdued the werewolves once and for all.

"Isn't it a little early in a relationship for us to be saving each other's lives?" Michael said with a half-laugh. He placed his hand under my head so it was no longer resting on the wood floor.

"Man, it burns so bad," I replied.

"Shhh," Michael said, placing his hand on my stomach where the fireball had hit me. He began chanting under his breath, and little by little I felt a coolness wash over me. It didn't take away the burning pain entirely, but I didn't feel like my insides were boiling anymore.

"Remind me to send your sister a thank-you note," I

replied as I struggled to sit up. I looked around the room. The place was destroyed. Scorch marks were burned into almost every surface. Tables and chairs were overturned. The couch was smoking. Not to mention the werewolves who were passed out on the floor.

In the entryway, the trio of witches stood. Mrs. Hendricks was hugging each one of them and fussing over their appearance.

"You can marry whoever you want. I don't care!" I heard Mrs. Hendricks say. I had a feeling she would never take her daughter for granted again. I also had a feeling that these three girls would be best friends for life.

True to her character, Nuala had taken off before I could properly thank her, and Lexi followed suit shortly after. If I knew my bestie, she wanted to be gone before the Clean-Up Crew (the Agency's supernatural scene cleaners) arrived because boy, they were going to be pretty ticked with the mess I left them to deal with.

The only thing I couldn't figure out is why the werewolves had been willingly assisting in killing off their own.

Michael had the answer to that. "Mary promised the stone to them when she was finished. She only wanted to use it to heal her mother. Then she was going to pass it on to them," he said.

"How do you know that?"

"Penny. She went back to the billiard hall for answers and managed to flirt the truth out of a shifter."

Ah, so Penny had been successful.

Michael helped me up.

"Case closed?" he asked me.

"Yep, case closed."

"If you want to take Mary in, my people will take it from here," I said.

"Are you sure?" Michael asked me.

"Positive."

"Well, at least let me call a uniform. They can arrest Mary, and I can give you a lift back to the city. You still have my keys, don't you?"

"Um ... they're in my purse, and I have no idea where that is right now."

"Okay, then I'll wait."

"Michael. I don't think it's a good idea. Listen—" Again, I was stuck between a rock and a hard place.

"What?" he asked.

But I couldn't bring myself to tell him the truth. I took the easy way out. "You don't really need your keys to start your car, do you? Head on home. I'll catch up with you later," I said, even though I knew there would be no later.

"Okay, later then." Michael turned to leave, but not before casting a look over his shoulder.

I replied with a weak smile. Sometimes my job really sucked.

With the scene under control and the Clean-Up Crew descending at any moment, I knew my time was up. I walked outside into the starry night and headed down to the water's edge. The lake was flat and calm, and I used that peace to center myself and speak the words that would send me home.

From this time I must depart
I've done my job and time can restart
Bring me home cosmos I ask thee
In my own time is where I need to be

MY STOMACH WAS STILL QUEASY, and the room wasn't completely in focus when a knock came at the front door. I placed my hand on the kitchen table to steady myself. Agatha rolled over and looked at me. She was already back asleep after sending her life-saving message.

The knock came once more.

"I swear on all things witchy, that had better not be Andrew," I said, taking a calming breath and walking to answer it.

I yanked the door open, ready to tell Andrew off, and stood there dumbstruck.

It was Michael.

"What? How?" I stammered.

"You think you're the only witch who's mastered time travel?" he said with a smile.

"What? No. It's just ..." I was at a loss for words.

"I had to see for myself where to find you. Oh, and to give you this." He leaned across the doorframe and kissed me. It was sweet and warm and had my heart doing a little pitter patter.

"See you around, Vee," he said as he stepped back and disappeared into thin air.

And darn it if I didn't wish it would be sooner rather than later.

<<<<>>>>
Hey Reader,
Do you like mystery games? What about a free story? Turn the page for your first clue!

SCAVENGER HUNT

We're going on a scavenger hunt!

Collect one code word in the back of each of the five Witch in Time Mysteries and unlock bonus content from your favorite time-traveling witches.

Your first code word is: **Time**

Good luck!

ARE YOU READY?

Dear Reader,

You've followed Vee Harper through the streets of Manhattan as she's tracked a missing person and fought of witches and shifters along the way--but that's nothing to the perils facing Felicia Octavia Geraldine Warner the Fourth, "Flick," is about to face in 1999.

Are you up for the journey?

Pack your bags because we're headed to London. A dead body has been discovered in the Old Bailey and it's going to take more than a little magic to solve this case.

Read Book 2 in the Witch in Time Mystery Series today!

ABOUT THE AUTHOR

I'm a mystery author with a soft spot for romance and humor, too. I love all things girlie with a dollop of danger, have a strong affinity for the color pink (especially in diamonds and champagne), and, not to brag, but chocolate and I are in a pretty serious relationship.

My books are fun and flirty, and feature smart and sassy sleuths. If you love books with a dash of spice and twist of whodunit, you're going to love my work!

ALSO BY STEPHANIE DAMORE

Beauty Secrets Series Order

Book One: Makeup & Murder

Book Two: Kiss & Makeup

Book Three: Eyeliner & Alibis

Book Four: Pedicures & Prejudice

Book Five: Beauty & Bloodshed

Book Six: Charm & Deception

Short Story: A Ring to Die For

Spirited Sweets Series Order

Book One: Bittersweet Betrayal

Book Two: Decadent Demise

Book Three: Red Velvet Revenge

Boxed Set: Spirited Sweets

Multi-Author Series

Better Witch Next Time

Mourning After